Praise for

GODS OF WANT

"These stories by the Taiwanese American author of the gutsy 2020 debut novel *Bestiary* are obsessed with the vagaries of emigration and adolescence. Populated by ghosts and spirits, they dissolve the rigidities of American life into a slipstream of folkloric myth and transform the familiar world into something wilder." —*The New York Times*

"Alert to the ways reality can buckle and contort, Chang conjures fiction that is almost fairytale-like, mythical, unsettling—yet at the same time blisteringly alive and un-apologetically queer.... The collection's compendiums of memories and myth are rife with consumption and desire, lifted by Chang's poetic sensibility." —*The Guardian*

"Chang has a special talent for forging history into myth and myth into present-day fiction.... *Gods of Want* is in some ways a fantasy of queer freedom. Its main characters, all Taiwanese or Chinese by birth or descent, are allowed to be who they are, to love and make love to whomever they choose." —*Los Angeles Times*

"Shifting between genres, modes, and degrees of gravity, the collection displays the young Taiwanese American author's striking inventiveness, both at the level of imagery and of language, as well as her cutting humor." —*Los Angeles Review of Books*

"[The] ability to take a common, decidedly earthbound, experience and transform it through her lens into a fantastical, otherworldly encounter shines in Chang's new book, the short-story collection *Gods of Want*.... Chang's writing reflects her gift as a lifelong listener of oral storytelling, especially from her mother and grandmothers, and her ability to synthesize new ideas with her own spin on language."

—*San Francisco Chronicle*

"These speculative, surreal short stories center the experiences of Asian American women: their bodies, relationships, identities, myths, and memories. Chang's trademark feminist fabulist style blends themes of queerness, ghosts, migration, the body, and more." —*Autostraddle*

"K-Ming Chang . . . is back with her signature precise and enthralling prose in this short-story collection. Asian American women are central to this collection as Chang explores their relationships to themselves, their bodies, and beyond.... Memory, myth, ghosts, and queerness float from these pages, further solidifying Chang's talent."

—*Shondaland*

"Chang wields words like almost no other writer I can think of: every sentence is hefty, exact, musical." —*Book Riot*

"Chang is incredibly skilled at writing about the body while weaving in myth, mystery, and earthly realities. These tales about the myriad relationships between women are no exception, and reading them is a whole body experience."

—*them*

"Lyrical and deliciously experimental . . . The hunger these characters have for life, for each other, is all so visceral it's impossible to walk away from. *Gods of Want* is one of those collections I know I'll find myself reaching for again and again, hungry for all the things I know it still has to tell me."

—*Heavy Feather*

"If you're looking for a jolt that will have your brain tingling and your heart fluttering, turn to *Gods of Want*, a delightfully provocative short story collection from K-Ming Chang that promises to keep you energized—and in awe—for days. . . . Wildly inventive."

—Fredericksburg *Free Lance-Star*

"These strange, eerie, and beautiful stories about queer Asian American women are full of choruses of dead cousins, the wisdom of aunts, troublesome widows, and girls discovering their bodies. Chang's prose is absolutely dazzling. Her words cast a spell that makes it feel like every story is a prose poem."

—*Book Riot*

"This is the real deal. . . . *Gods of Want* actually tries to be new, to see what a short story can hold. The collection is, refreshingly, very strange. . . . The line-to-line pleasures are too frequent to categorize. Turning to any arbitrary page will reveal some compelling image or slimy, lush description. . . . Chang's characters, like all her stories in *Gods of Want*, are hungry for meat and blood—and for love, identity, a world. None of these hungers is metaphorical. Each is simply, magically, another kind of wanting."

—*Slant*

"K-Ming Chang's stories vibrate with energy, lyricism, and the hysteria that comes from the crushing weight of history. As a collection of stories, *Gods of Want* spans generations— orbiting relationships between women, their bodies, their ancestors, and their wild environments. There is an aura of mythic simultaneity in the work as deceased ancestors, immigration trauma, environmental anxiety, and queer relationships collapse into poignant, uncanny narratives. Chang's writing style is musical, heady, fabulist, and straddles the line between grotesque and lovely.... *Gods of Want* is a glitteringly surreal collection that flirts with genres like magical realism, humor, and horror but defies the very categorization it attempts—some things *can't* be measured, only experienced.... *Gods of Want* is a culmination of that inventiveness—a full community of voices infused with their own complexities, absurdities, and desire." —*The Journal*

"From the author of the acclaimed novel *Bestiary* comes this original, queer, hilarious and brave collection of stories centering the lives, loves, labors and longings of Asian American women." —*Ms.* magazine

"The fierce little machines found in the Taiwanese American writer K-Ming Chang's first collection, *Gods of Want*... [are] possessed of a powerful hunger, a drive to metabolize the recognizable features of a familiar world and transform them into something wilder, and achingly alive.... A voracious, probing collection, proof of how exhilarating the short story can be in the hands of a writer who, as one of her narrators puts it, 'somehow...made every word sound like want.'" —*The New York Times*

"Chang's lush prose is full of decadent-but-icky imagery."

—*Metro Silicon Valley*

"*Gods of Want* both widens and calcifies the expansiveness of [Chang's] range. A blessed many authors are doing this today—and so many of them are queer—but Chang is singular amongst us all. She is really fucking good at her job. . . . New work from Chang is a cause for celebration—a holiday in its own right—and it's also a reminder of the infinite possibilities on the page. That she's able to conjure so many pathways—without insisting on answers or conclusions, only more ways of being—is nothing short of marvelous."

—*Electric Literature*

"K-Ming Chang's inspired mix of magic and realism returns in full fabulist force in this new collection of short stories, the follow-up to her critically acclaimed debut novel *Bestiary*. The stories are eclectic . . . and united by Chang's fascination with the queer and quotidian in her characters' worlds. That the author is so young and her insights so piercing speaks to not only her talents, but the value in drawing from our myths, elders, and histories."

—*Esquire*

"*Gods of Want* . . . reaffirms [Chang's] place as one of our most enchanting storytellers today. . . . From every first sentence, she has you hooked. . . . So much of the joy of reading K-Ming Chang's stories is in her ability to constantly surprise. . . . Every sentence bites down."

—*Literary Hub*

"Explosive and bizarre . . . Chang glides effortlessly between the shocking and quotidian, demanding attention, deserving applause."

—*Booklist* (starred review)

"Composed of 16 short stories that explore the immigrant experience, this book traces a line from old worlds to new worlds by means of the bloody umbilical cords that stretch between them. . . . The ease with which the various narrators shift into poetic transcendence in their workaday descriptions coupled with the linguistic flexibility of non-native idioms repurposed for a new English in a new world is as much a part of the storytelling as the stories themselves. All this together leaves the reader with a lingering sense that language, as well as life, is infinitely adaptable, no matter the ground on which it is given to grow. Lurid, funny, strange, and deftly sorrowing—an important new voice."

—*Kirkus Reviews* (starred review)

"In the genre of feminine madness, these stories are to be worshiped. They are fearless, hysterical, violent yet full of grace. Each sentence escalates toward devastating, poetic insight about our bodies, about cultural demands both treasured and feared, and about what makes being alive a terror and a joy."

—VENITA BLACKBURN,
author of *How to Wrestle a Girl*

"No one writes like K-Ming Chang. Wise, energetic, funny, and wild, *Gods of Want* displays a boundless imagination anchored by the weight of ancestors and history. These stories sing, a true force to behold."

—KALI FAJARDO-ANSTINE, author of
Sabrina & Corina and *Woman of Light*

"The beauty, humor, and brilliance throughout *Gods of Want* shines brightly from story to story—Chang's collection is constantly illuminating and thoroughly astounding. K-Ming Chang's mastery of language, and the boundlessness of her empathy, make for a strange, hilarious, and unforgettable read. *Gods of Want* is a gift and a masterclass, a stunning and moving work by one of our most brilliant authors."

—BRYAN WASHINGTON,
author of *Lot* and *Memorial*

"These stories glitter and pulse, announcing Chang, with her second book, as a front-runner of innovation anew. Full of mythic desire, joy, and pain disguised as the other, and navigating the precarious balance of how to belong to a land while still belonging to oneself, *Gods of Want* is bursting with language and images so striking, so sure of their own strength, I found myself stunned. The worlds and characters depicted in these pages are original, strange, sometimes horrific, and all the more gorgeous because of it."

—DANTIEL W. MONIZ,
author of *Milk Blood Heat*

BY K-MING CHANG

Bestiary
Gods of Want

GODS
OF
WANT

GODS
OF
WANT

Stories

K-MING CHANG

ONE WORLD
NEW YORK

Published in the United States by One World,
an imprint of Random House, a division of Penguin
Random House LLC, New York.

ONE WORLD and colophon æregistered trademarks of
Penguin Random House LLC.

Originally published in hardcover in the United States by One World,
an imprint of Random House, a division of Penguin
Random House LLC, in 2022.

The following stories were originally published in differ ent form: "Mandarin
Speakers" in *DREGINALD*, "The Chorus of Dead Cousins" in *McSweeney's
Quarterly Concern*, "Meals for Mourners" in *Nashville Review*, "Eating Pussy"
and "Homophone" in *New Delta Review*, "Auntland" in *Sine Theta Magazine*,
"Dykes" in *Sinister Wisdom*, and "Nine-Headed Birds" in *VIDA Review*.

LIBRARY OF CONGRESS CATALOGING-IN-PUBLICATION DATA
Names: Chang, K-Ming, author.
Title: Gods of want : stories / by K-Ming Chang.
Description: New York : One World, [2023]
Identifiers: LCCN 2021019321(print) | LCCN 2021019322 (ebook) |
ISBN 9780593241608 (trade paperback) | ISBN 9780593241592 (ebook)
Classification: LCC PS3603.H35733 G63 2022 (print) | LCC PS3603.H35733
(ebook) | DDC 813/.6—dc23
LC record available at https://lcc.loc.gov/2021019321
LC ebook record available at https://lccn.loc.gov/2021019322

Printed in Canada on acid-free paper

oneworldlit.com

1st Printing

Book design by Jo Anne Metsch

FOR

Amy, Annina, Kyle, and Pik-Shuen

Contents

MOTHERS

Auntland

I had an aunt who went to the dentist and asked to get her tongue pulled. *We only do teeth,* the dentist said, but did it anyway. She took her tongue home in a jar and flushed it down the toilet and years later a fisherman in Half Moon Bay made the evening news, waving my aunt's tongue like a flag at the end of his pole. The police are still looking for the body it belonged to. I had an aunt who worked at the Oriental Buffet and stole us a live crab, which my other aunt boiled alive, and when I tried to crack the legs with my teeth the way they did, one of my molars fractured into five and my other aunt, not that other aunt but this other other aunt, spent the rest of the night tweezing tooth-shrapnel out of my gums. I had an aunt who told me not to get braces because it would set off the metal detector at airports and trigger the German shepherds to run out and tackle me and the agents would confiscate my teeth and replace them with rubber bullets and interrogate my mouth with their tongues. I had an aunt who took me to Great America while my mother was at an immigration interview.

This aunt refused to get on a roller coaster even though that's
what we paid for. When I told her to get on, she said, *The only
time I'll get off the ground is if I'm on an airplane or become an
angel.* And I told her she'd never become an angel because I
saw her kiss a woman that time we were at Walmart buying
four-ply toilet paper for my mother, who was in the throes of
stress diarrhea, induced partially by her upcoming immigration interview and partially because I told her the officers
would test if she was truly American by feeding her strawberry soft serve and timing her digestion. I said that's why it's
called *passing a test*—because they catch what passes out of
your body. If it's liquid, they don't let you into the country. So
my mother went out and bought two half-gallons of Breyers
vanilla to train her body to convert milk into bone and not
brown silk. Anyway, my aunt locked me in the parked car,
which I said was illegal in America—you can't even lock dogs
in the car—and she walked up to the woman who had been
following us while we shopped, a woman I'd recognized from
the temple where we prayed to save my grandfather's polyga-
mist soul, and kissed her. Kissed her so hard, my own lips
shriveled like salted slugs. I had an aunt who gave me the lingerie catalog because there were coupons printed in it, though
none of us would ever wear underwear with jewels or lace,
because jewels and lace need to be worn on the outside so that
everyone knows you can afford them. I cut the bottom halves
off the women for no reason. At school we watched an Oprah
interview where a white woman tells Oprah how she stopped
her attacker: by peeing on him. I had an aunt who peed on me
one time we shared a mattress. She'd been in the country five
months and when I woke up she was trying to shroud the stain
with a towel. She said she'd dreamed of being back on the island, peeing onto the roots of a camphor tree that didn't grow

unless it was given water directly from a body. I imagined I was that tree: I grew because my aunts were watering me. I had an aunt who cut my hair for years, until she got early-onset something, some disease named after a man, and then she went around cutting people's earlobes on purpose, sneaking up behind them with her scissors and shearing off the tips like bits of shrubbery, and for years every time I sensed something behind me, a pigeon or the gym teacher or rain, I assumed it was her. I covered my ears in my sleep, could never hear in my dreams. I had an aunt who swathed cellophane candy wrappers around the heads of flashlights and shined the beams onto my ceiling before I fell asleep, telling me it was the northern lights, and when I asked her what even caused the northern lights, she said it was the sky having bad breath. The sky spitting its stars like teeth. When night is the color of all my aunts letting down their hair, I remember I have another aunt who got all her teeth bashed in on a bus. She doesn't remember the man who did it, just woke up at the end of the line with the bus driver slapping her awake, telling her she better learn some English, so she did. I had an aunt who said chewing orchid petals is the only sure form of birth control. I had another aunt who said dying is the only sure form of birth control. I had an aunt who wanted to name her daughter *Dog* because that's what Americans love most of all, dogs, and how many movies are there about American dogs that must find their way home to their families? And how many of those dogs die, percentage-wise? And can't a name give her the odds she'll need? I had an aunt who saw me kiss a girl in the booth of a Burger King and said, *I knew it. I knew you were supposed to be born a son.* I had an aunt who pulled me out of my mother by a jellied ankle and said, *Of course she's born backward, everyone in this family is.* I had an aunt whose baby died in its sleep so soundlessly, she didn't believe in its death. She dressed it, rocked it, petted its head, not letting us take the body away, until one night we tricked her, replacing the baby with a Costco frozen baked potato. She mothered the potato instead, wrapped it in a blanket, pretended it was safe in the custody of her touch. I had an aunt who died in a drunk-driving accident, in a sober-driving accident, in a suicide, in a typhoon, in the middle of the day while blow-drying her hair, in the evening while opening a window, in the morning while hiking to the family grave, in an attempt to get away from her husband, in an attempt to get away from her father, in an attempt to leave the country, in an attempt to get into another one, in an attempt to get her nose done, in an attempt to love a son, in an attempt to outrun a river, in an attempt to reincarnate as rain. I had an aunt who cracked an egg on my forehead when I made fun of her accent. I had an aunt who did my hair before school every morning, marinating my braid in egg yolk and butter, saying I'd smell like an American. I had an aunt who wiped her ass with her birth certificate and another one who failed her immigration test because she named Colonel Sanders as a founding father. I had an aunt who made sausage out of wild squirrels she shot in her yard, and when I said those squirrels probably had diseases, she held me to the chair until I ate every link. I had an aunt who stood outside the bathroom and listened to me shit, saying she could divine the shape of my future based on how my shit fell: whether it sank right away, whether it floated like petals or sang in the water or became a fish. I had an aunt who never married and told me men are magpies: They want anything that shines. What shines: blood, a bruise like an eye patch, a lake, salt, a window, dew, sweat on a girl's collarbone, my aunts pledging allegiance to the moon. I had an aunt who massaged my elbows when I cried and said the heart is a hinge, to live it must bend. I had an aunt who said I should carry a rock in my palm until it's the same temperature as my body, and then I should talk to the rock as if she is inside it. She says we should all learn to listen through other skins. I had an aunt who said home is the temperature of an armpit. I had an aunt who never let me turn on the heat, because if we don't pay for the sun's light or warmth we shouldn't pay for heat or electricity, so she tucked my hands under her armpits and pretended she was a hen and I was the egg, swaddled in wings, swimming inside a shell of light, waiting to break to birth to sing.

The Chorus of Dead Cousins

I warned my wife about them. They volunteered as our bridesmaids and came dressed in nets, fishhooks in their eyes, alive. They glued thorns into all the flower arrangements and stepped on my wife's dress until it tore, baring her ass, and then they used the veil to run around outside and catch hairy moths in its gauze. They knotted my tie into a noose and hung it from the church ceiling like a chandelier, but I didn't know how to kick them out once they were there. They brought gifts, fistfuls of worms and a downed telephone pole. They ate the cake and told us it was dry and asphalt-like. They farted in the minister's face and shattered a stained-glass window depicting a nativity scene and said it was our fault Mary was beheaded and baby Jesus was crushed into an anthill of sand. They stole the cutlery, and I later found all the salad forks stabbed into the trees along the street, sap rusting on the trunks. When the ceremony moved outside, some of them attempted to straddle clouds and deliver a speech, but then it started to rain, a rain that fell thick as unpinned hair, tangling everywhere.

My wife said she'd never known I had so many dead family members, that when I'd mentioned my cousins she'd thought I meant a few, and I said you should see how many are still living. My mother always used to joke: *In this family, it's one in the ground and a dozen more dangling from the trees, waiting to be plucked. It's one buried and a hundred more begging to be born.*

It was only a week after the wedding that my wife threatened to leave me, claiming that the chorus of dead cousins was straining her sleep, dicing her dreams fine with their fingers like pocketknives. It was true they were intrusive, carving out our windows and replacing them with panes of molten sugar that the raccoons came to lick at night, waking us with the drumbeat of their tongues. It was true that they liked to get into bed with us, six of their bodies sardined between us, and that most of my cousins kicked under the sheets as if trying to surface from sleep. We woke with black shins and rubber ribs. Sometimes I woke up with my lungs hung upside down in my chest, and my cousins were in the closet laughing as I tried to breathe while doing a headstand. But still, I told my wife, they were family, they didn't have bodies to go back to, and so she let me keep kitty-litter boxes in the corner of the room so they wouldn't wet our bed, and she let me teach them how to change our lightbulbs so at least they were helpful: Because they could ascend and descend at will, it was easy for them to reach the ceiling.

For a while I thought I had finally tamed them, and though they occasionally chased the mailman or tore out our plumbing, unrolling a flood as proudly as a flag, they knew not to do anything truly deranged, like removing their entrails and playing lasso-the-cowboy with them, or trying to flush one another down the toilet, or plucking daddy longlegs off our walls and training them to wrestle each other. I was proud of their restraint and of how well they dressed in death, sewing their own skirts from grass clippings and stolen curtains, and at least now they were odorless and clean, not like when they were living and smelled like gasoline and wet knives and lotto scratchers.

Then one day my wife got up and looked in the mirror and saw that one of the dead cousins had swapped all her teeth for the red-dyed shells of melon seeds. *Okay*, I said finally, *I'll get rid of them.*

We need an exterminator, my wife said, but all the ones I called were men who said they didn't deal with what was already dead. I explained that I didn't need them killed, I just needed them to go on vacation for a little while, to stalk another surname for a month or two, to reincarnate maybe. My call was cut off when the chorus of dead cousins severed the phone service by becoming brooms of wind, sweeping out all the telephone lines on our street.

That night in bed, with the chorus of dead cousins dog-curled at our feet, my wife said what we needed was an evacuation. She was always speaking in the vocabulary of storms, of evacuations and casualties and degrees of damage. She had the spine of a storm too: There was a stillness to her center, but her limbs churned the air, choreographing wreckage wherever she went. At night I liked to wake up and watch her wrestle with her own skin, snaking all over the bed, navigating the night into her mouth and eating it.

My wife is a professional storm chaser. When we met, there was a card pinned to her sleeve that said SEVERE-WEATHER

PHOTOGRAPHER. I told her that was a white-woman thing to do, chasing storms on purpose. We were in the lobby of a dentist's office and she was thumbing through a copy of *National Geographic,* an issue on the Tornado Alley of the Midwest, and without asking my name she turned to me and showed me the page with her photograph printed on it.

My photograph didn't make the cover, she said, *but they paid me eighty bucks.* I looked down at the page, her wrists a silver frame. The photograph was a full page, and splayed across it was a tornado like a ringlet of black hair, almost too intentionally arranged. It tapered down to the width of a single hair, and at the base of it, in the distance, was a thumbprint-sized town. The tornado was either leaving it or heading toward it, but it was impossible to tell which, and already it seemed implausible that anyone had ever been born there, born in a city that could be distilled into a disaster.

I looked away from the woman's hands, the fluorescence of that photograph. I didn't remember seeing a sky in it, but there had to be a sky for there to be a storm: There had to be an origin for ruin. I was suddenly jealous of that tornado, the way it tangoed on the page, the way her hand ran down its length like a spine. The photo was taken from the perspective of someone who loved it, and I wanted to be captured that way, to be chased from my body.

Have you ever been near something like this? she asked. A typhoon, I told her, when I was little in Taiwan and all my cousins were still living. My ama was perpetually breathless and lived with only one lung, and my agong was a former soldier who slept with his gun, until one night we heard it go off in his mouth. My mother sent me to the island when I was four so she could stay in California and make money. She said she would send for me in a year, but the years bred like cicadas and outnumbered my memories, and by the time I was ten I no longer remembered her face and had to look at my own in the water of the well and circle the parts of me that were hers.

The year my mother sent for me, with no more money than when she sent me away, one of my cousins jumped into the well and had to be pulled out by her hair the next morning. She was in training to be a hairdresser, and she liked to use me as practice, clamping my head between her knees until I cried. Always, when she released me, I was a new species, my hair sculpted into antlers or siphoned into braids or cut short as a boy's, which made my ama cry but seduced me into spending weeks looking down at myself in the well, wanting to jump just to get closer to that girl in the water.

The typhoons came in herds every summer, but there was only one I remembered, the one that had my name. It was August and the bulls were being manufactured into oxen. The cousins did this by tying the bull's balls together and using a meat mallet to mash them. This was the only way to tame them. I knew how to plug my ears with mud so that I wouldn't hear the moaning of those bulls. When the typhoon came, it rained hands, little hands and big hands, soft hands and callused hands, and the sea's waves were hands too, woman-hands that plucked the roof off Ama's house and reached in and confiscated her, tucking her into the back pocket of the sky.

That's not a typhoon, the woman in the waiting room said, *that's a tsunami.* I told her she hadn't heard the point of the story. There was something about that tornado photograph that made me offer my losses, and I thought she might bare hers too. But instead she looked down at her lap—for a photographer, she had surprising difficulty looking directly at anything—and said, *I bet I've captured every kind of disaster.* She bent her head, baring her nape. I thought of the way mother cats carried their kittens by biting their napes and swinging them around, and I wanted to know what my teeth would do to that tender estate.

What about an earthquake, I said, and this made her pause. *You can't take a picture of an earthquake,* she said, still not looking at me. *You can only take a picture of the aftermath.* The buckled knees of buildings, the streets razored with cracks.

Have you ever been in one? I said, wanting her to look at me. I wished we weren't in a waiting room, side by side: I wanted to rearrange the place so every seat was facing another, so I was the horizon of the room.

She laughed and said of course she'd been in one, *this is California, aren't you from here,* and I said I didn't know how it felt. I slept through earthquakes, or I was always in the air when they happened, flying back to some funeral for some cousin somewhere, dead for reasons that were always deemed natural, though I knew which ones had husbands, which ones had medications, which ones had histories and debts and seventh-story windows.

The dental assistant called her name—even her name sounded like a storm warning, a single vowel—and I decided to stand up as if it belonged to me. She had a surname like mine and a father from Shanghai who I later learned was *estranged,* a term she taught me. She watched me stand, her head jerking up, but she didn't stop me from substituting for her. It was my first time going to a dentist, and I thought for some reason I'd have to undress. Before I was sent back to my mother, one of my cousins claimed that all doctors were perverts and just wanted to strip you naked and touch everything you didn't yet have a name for. When that cousin went to get an abortion, the doctor told her to insert six cloves of garlic into her vagina, and when she used chilies instead—the garlic

hadn't yet grown in—we all woke up that night to the sound
of her shouting. She ran out of the house and waded waist-
deep into the river and soaked like that for a full day before the
pain was put out.

The dentist was a woman with forehead lines as clear and
deep as if they were plowed, and she reminded me of one of
my cousins, who taught me to climb trees and lick my own
skinned knees. But the difference was that the dentist had perfect teeth, a bright cavalry of canines, and when her hands
were in my mouth I tried not to think of biting them off. No
one in my family had teeth by the age of fifty. Their molars
were martyred one by one to stones, ox bones, peach pits, fists.

Swallow, the dentist said, her hands clamped on either side
of my neck. *This is a test*, she said, while the fluorescent light
flirted with me. But I couldn't swallow when I was told to, so I
thought instead of the woman in the waiting room and the
dust redirected into a tornado, dusking the air between us. My
spit thickened into a seed and I swallowed finally, plotting to
be a tree. I'd read somewhere that all photographs were self-
portraits—probably a man had said that—and I wondered
where she was in that photo, if she was the funnel or the sky
or the town that wasn't named anywhere, not even in the caption.

After my appointment, my mouth still tasting of latex, I
found the woman sitting in the waiting room. I apologized for
cutting her in line, and she told me not to worry, that she was
dreading what she'd come for. *I waited for you*, she said. In her
palms, she carried a thimble-sized plastic pirate chest. When I
sat down next to her again, she lifted the box and opened it,
flashing me the tooth inside, a rot-speckled molar. Outside the
context of her mouth, the tooth looked like a tadpole, a shifting species, not yet adapted to air. *A quick extraction*, she said.

They numbed me. The left side of her face was lagging behind the right. Her smile was quicksand, one side sinking into the other, tongue mud-sliding over her teeth.

When the woman took me home with her, I recognized the neighborhood of teeth-bright houses and metallic sidewalks, the roads circling themselves: a place designed to protect. Where every house was chaperoned by trees and the only litter was leaves. My mother used to take me to the houses she kept clean, houses like these. While I ate worms in the yard and sucked on doorknobs, my mother would walk through the house one last time, searching for strands of black hair we had shed, collecting them before we left.

In bed, the woman tugged my hair, called me by another name. I recognized it as mine only in retrospect, answering to it too late. Her hand traced my spine as if trying to find a light switch along it. A flick to flood me. She closed the curtains, the lacy kind designed not to defy the light but to dress it. But the sky shut itself off, and in the dark all I could see was the slick of her chin, her tongue paddling the dark.

When we were lying side by side, I started telling her a story she didn't believe, about my twin cousins in Yilan who bit their wrists open in prison and bled out. When she asked me what I did for a living, I said I didn't do anything for the living. I only did things for the dead. *I'm a conductor,* I said, joking. She turned on her side, curling inward, and said, *Of music? Heat? Electricity?* She slid her hand between my thighs and laughed, her palm griddled by the warmth of me. For the first time, I looked at her teeth closely, wondering if she was still numb on one side, if she could taste what her tongue had done.

Of a chorus, I said, though my cousins were dormant then, not yet tailing me so closely. *Clouds are conductors,* she said, ignoring me. She told me that every storm has an anatomy and that the root of a tornado is located in the sky, anchored to the clouds and not the ground. *It's our nature,* she said, *to assume that things grow upward.* She turned onto her back again and lifted her arm straight to the ceiling, told me to imagine it was a tornado descending. *Is it true you're supposed to hide in a bathtub?* I asked.

Instead of answering, she got up in the dark and ran to the bathroom. When the tub was shimmering full, we got in together and fumbled for each other underwater, sharing one rope of breath between us. My mother used to corral me into the bathtub while she cleaned the bedrooms, and when I crawled out to escape, she plucked me up and put me back. Her hand descending like something divine. Even now, underwater with my legs laced around a stranger, I expected a hand to reach down and remove me from desire.

In the daytime, she researched tornado season and I worked at a seafood-preparation plant, soaking the beheaded shrimp in trays of brine, jabbing air holes into Styrofoam boxes so the crabs could survive flight.

Two months before our wedding, she took me to a restaurant called the Whale's Mouth, a seafood chain where you could select a live lobster from a light-blanched aquarium in the window. I told her if she wanted a live lobster, I could bring her one from the factory, one of the extra-limbed mutants we plucked off the conveyor belt. We could split it, eat a tail each. I told her this restaurant was appropriating my people's culture of eating only what you can kill yourself. She told me to stop complaining.

In the ladies' bathroom of the Whale's Mouth, where the door was shaped like a cartoon molar, my cousins walked out of the stalls and stood behind me while I rinsed my hands. They were dark and slick as racehorses, striding out on their hands and knees. Some of them I recognized from Yilan. Others were cousins my mother brought along on her housecleaning route, their surgical gloves swinging like milked udders. I tallied their teeth, cleaned their knees. All of them told me they disapproved of me going to the dentist, because dentists were scammers. As proof, one of them opened his mouth and showed me where his molars were crowned with gold. *Fake gold*, he said, *the hard stuff. I told my mother to take my teeth when I was dead. She knocked them out with a sock full of stones, and in the end they couldn't even pay off my funeral. A scam.*

I told him that his experience with the dentist was one incident, an outlier. The rest of the cousins said I was starting to rhyme with her, that woman, my soon-to-be wife, who spoke about things like charts and diagrams and latitudes. One of them turned his head and spat on the tile floor and I remembered him, the one who laughed at me because I thought pineapples grew on trees before my mother sent me to Yilan. *You probably think babies grow inside men*, he said, and later that summer my ama caught him with a boy from Success Cliff. She tied him to the trunk of a tree and all night I heard him yelling for us to cut him loose.

After I left the island, I got a call from Ama saying he ran away, which I knew meant he was dead and I shouldn't ask how. I cradled the landline in my palm, remembering the baby pineapple he plucked for me in the fields behind Ama's house.

It was smaller than his palm, candled in his hands, its rind not yet yellow-spiked. *This is the heart,* he said, coring it with one stroke. *The part you can't eat.* He gave me a wedge of flesh, the juice cording down my throat. When I asked for more, he gave me his half and gnawed on the heart, sawing at it with his teeth. Ama told me that only poor people eat the heart of a pineapple, which is fibrous and flavorless as wood. Your tongue carries the splinters for the rest of its life, unable to speak anything complete.

The chorus began that year when I was twelve. It was the summer I came home to California and told my mother, in summary, a story about testicles. My cousin in Yilan, the oldest one, who practiced castrating bulls by swinging his hammer into peaches, liked to stand beside my futon at night and cradle his balls in his hands. *Open your mouth,* he told me. *Gross,* I said. *No.* He said, *Fine,* but the next night he came with the hammer and said, *Open, open.* When my mother heard this story, she told me not to talk about my cousins anymore. They were attracted to shit, she said, like flies, and they died at the same rate. Every time someone called with news of another one running away, my mother folded a fast-food napkin into a lotus flower and burned it.

Lotuses, she said, float on the surface of water, free of the mud that makes them. *You should learn something from this,* she said, marrying her match to the paper petals. In the bathroom of the Whale's Mouth, I redirected my dead cousins to the seafood display outside. What I knew about my cousins: They were always hungry, necklaced in tongues. While they reached inside the aquarium and snatched up the lobsters, distracting all the waiters and causing a minor flood, I tugged my fiancée outside and drove us home. She was upset about not getting to eat her lobster, but I told her that escaping the cho-

rus of dead cousins meant all crustaceans must be left behind.
It was a small sacrifice.

There has to be somewhere better for them, my wife said. They
could be adopted into good families, ones that would love them
better dead than they were ever loved while living. I agreed
and tried to disguise them as dogs, looping them into leashes,
but it was evident at the adoption center that they were walking on two legs and owned opposable thumbs.

She was willing to tolerate them for another month, but it
was nearly tornado season and now was the time for her to
focus and prepare. In March she plotted a path east to Okla-
homa and then south to Texas, packing her parents' Jeep with
dehydrated-food packets and water bottles and battery-
powered lanterns and binoculars and her camera with its zoom
lens that looked like the barrel of a gun. I told her I would
come with her, and she said, *Not with them.*

If anything can deter the chorus of dead cousins, I told her,
it's a tornado. They wouldn't dare come close to anything that
could cleave them into steam. My wife didn't believe me, but
she agreed to take me anyway, and when the June heat began
to circle the city like a noose, we drove away. The dead cousins
watched from the driveway, waving and weeping, begging me
to take them along. One of them was flapping his shirt at me
like a handkerchief, and I wondered where they had learned
to perform this kind of goodbye. From an old movie, maybe,
about soldiers forced to depart the countries they'd conquered.
There was something staged about their farewell, and I knew
they were just waiting for us to leave.

My wife said they were fluent only in the vocabulary of
senseless destruction, but weeks before we left, I saw the cous-

ins in the backyard with shovels. They were standing in a row like soldiers, and when I asked what they were doing, they said, *We're making you a moat.* They told me that it was the season of wildfires and they wanted to make sure the flames wouldn't find us, and then they bent their heads in unison and began to dig. Some of them dug with their hands or the dishes of their detached kneecaps. All night, I could hear the sound of them knuckling into the earth.

I recognized the face of the cousin who'd initiated the digging. It was unusual for me to differentiate them, and even I began to call them by their cause of death, the way my wife did. This was the Cousin Whose Blood Did Not Clot. When she moved in with my ama, husbandless and with two children, we had to wrap the corners of the table in newspaper, bury the knives, dull our own nails by biting them short. We were afraid of touching her, because her blood was like a ribbon that could only be reeled out in one piece, one river length, unable to knot. One day we found her faceup in the pineapple fields, a man's machete in her chest and all of her blood outside her body, a red shroud we tugged over her face.

When my wife and I drove away from the duplex, my bloodless cousin was the one who cried the loudest. She hung herself up in the doorway, swinging her body like a bell. As we left, I tugged on her voice like a thread and it kept unraveling, following us east through Nevada. My dead cousins must have hijacked the sound track for our drive, because every time I turned on the radio, I heard a symphony of cicadas and clacking lobster claws. The Jeep swelled with cane-field smoke and I kept opening the windows, coaxing it out. Ahead, the road curved like a rib, and I imagined my cousins standing at the sides, thumbs up to ask for a ride. But all we passed was desert, delayed rain, blond dirt. Cacti spined the sky. When it was my turn to drive, I swerved off the road every two miles, mistaking a dust devil for a child. *Relax,* my wife said, placing her hand on the steering wheel to steady it, but I wasn't accustomed to this kind of wind. Wind dancing the dust, erecting it into walls.

In the desert, the towns were stitched farther apart and the dust barricaded our windshield. Even the landscape was illegible. The road ahead seemed to hinge, folding over us, but my wife told me it was just a mirage. My wife held a walkie-talkie in both hands, as if it were a holy object, and through the static of my cousins I heard the other storm chasers reporting the sky's condition: *Cloud of debris,* they said. *Hail in the absence of rain.*

It's coming, she said. The sky was purpling, either because it was evening or because it was full of pregnant clouds, each as round and bruised as a plum. A handful of wind-whisked pebbles rained down on me, and for a second I thought maybe my cousins were here, that this whole thing was a setup just to scare me: the sky, the static, the stolen sun. My wife said we should drive off-road and into the dusted fields, aiming to get underneath those clouds. She stood at the edge of the road with her hands offered out, waiting to catch something. The binoculars around her neck seemed comical: The clouds were huge as houses, all the lights shut off inside them.

My wife returned to the Jeep, sitting in the driver's seat. I stood beside it, watching her through the window. *This is your chance to see what I see,* she said, and I remembered that first time we were in bed, when she'd explained all the preparations necessary to get close to death and deny it. I wanted to tell her that some people don't need to get closer to death. They are born inside it and will never leave.

Can you taste it? she said, and I climbed in beside her. The clouds behind her were retracting, leaning back on their haunches, hungry. I tasted the sky's rim of sugar, smelled a cane field on fire. She was right: Storms had a smell, just like a body. *Let's go,* she said. *Let's get closer.* I buckled myself into the passenger seat, braced myself against the window. Out in the dust fields, there were other Jeeps sewn in a line like ants, other women waiting for the wind like kin.

She steered us into the fields, and though the land was flat, the Jeep startled me out of my seat. I wanted to ask whose land this was, if we were trespassing, but realized no one else was worrying. Ahead, a cloud extended its legs, two ropes of smoke groping for the ground, braiding back together. Beside me, my wife's hands on the wheel were shaking. It was a breech birth, the sky severed from any source of light, the cloud dragging its umbilical cord along the ground. *What is it,* my wife whispered, still driving. The other Jeeps ahead of us were scattering, scurrying away, but we kept going straight.

The tornado drilled into the ground. Dust beat on our windshield and broke it, glass basking on our laps. When it bent over us, the tornado was brighter than any of my teeth. It had a face. It was made of faces, eyeholes and mouth-holes perforating the funnel. My cousins singing with the entire sky as their skin, their mask. The dust digressed into limbs, dancing out of the debris, lashing out at the landscape. They were laughing, my dust-cousins, outgrowing their borrowed skin. I waited for their mouths to make a choir around us, sucking us into their stomach, but instead they grew upward. The Jeep was rocking with the force of their laughter, and my wife held up her camera. Hands shaking, she stood up in her seat, the canvas roof of the Jeep already shredded. When the camera's flash flooded every field with white water, I reached out and covered her lens with both hands. *Don't capture them*, I wanted to say. *Let them take the sky.*

The tornado splintered, torn into tissues of wind. Into the dark, I called my cousins' names. I called them home. My wife ducked into her seat, trying to ditch the wind. The air was so clotted with dust, I couldn't see her face, could only feel her fingers knotting around my wrist, tethering me to my seat. But I flung her off and ran out, the dust scouring my eyes bright. All around me, the wind rippled the fields like flags and the dust rose again, crusting into bodies. I told them to come down. *It isn't safe*, I said. *There will be storms.* But they hovered, constellations of dirt. They crowded my mouth, pretending to be salt. *Fine. Be that way*, I said, but every word was spat dust, another cousin leaving my body. Their names populating my tongue into a pincushion. I remembered the cousin who showed me the wood-splintered heart of a pineapple, how most people discard it but it was our duty to digest it. I opened my mouth, touching my tongue to sweet dust.

Xífù

I don't mean I want her to die. I'm just saying, what kind of woman pretends to kill herself six times? I'm saying that she loves to pretend. Some women are like that. They don't know what real means. Like that neighbor I had back on the island who pretended she was pregnant for three whole years. Her belly was a sack of guavas, all lumps, and she really thought no one would be able to tell. One of the neighborhood boys punched her in the belly to prove to his friends she wasn't actually pregnant, and all the guavas came rolling out the bottom of her dress and down the road. Juice sprayed everywhere and greenmeat jellied between her feet. And that woman cried about it too. She cried so hard and so long that the sea came forward and punched her out for spending so much of its salt. Some women will mourn anything, even things that haven't been born. I know a story about another woman on the island who impregnated a goat. In the dream, the woman masturbated—don't believe anyone who says she's never touched herself, she's probably touched herself

with all kinds of things, a karaoke microphone, an assort-
ment of vacuum-cleaner attachments, a fake jade statue of
Guanyin—and then offered her salted palm to her goat,
which licked it clean with its tongue.

Three months later, the goat got big in the belly and the
woman cut it open. Inside, there was a baby. She raised it all by
herself. The baby walked on all fours for its whole life, even
when it was a girl, and you can imagine what the boys thought
of her. They probably mounted her like a dog on the street.
The goatgirl had a baby every four days, I swear. That's the
story I heard. And she ate grass too. Her mouth was always
grazing the ground. What I always wanted to know was what
happened to the goat after it got cut open? How did they cook
it? Kebabs? Goat dumplings? Spit-roasting the whole thing?

That's why I told my daughter not to marry a man whose
mother is alive. Best if the mother is a goat or dead. That's the
only requirement I have: Don't marry a man with an origin.
Set his family on fire. But she tells me it's okay, that she'll
marry no one's son because she's a lesbian, and I'm so jealous I
could kick her in front of a car, the way I once did to the neighbor's pit bull when it shat maggots on my feet. There aren't
even any cars that come down our street anymore—they
stopped coming since the police roadblocked the strip mall.
They busted that massage place in the plaza, said it was full of
Chinese prostitutes. I called the newspaper to clarify: I'm Taiwanese. I used to work there. At night I slept with all the other
women, some from the mainland and some from the island
and some from other islands too small for even the sea to know
them. We slept in that hot back room, folding away all the tables and knotting together like a litter of pigs. The tatami
mats were plastic and gave me rashes, but sometimes it was
okay too, sometimes I liked hearing those women breathing

all around me, all the heat in our bodies enough to burn down the building.

I ask my daughter how you even become a lesbian and she says, first, I have to reject the male gaze. So I tell her the story of my father, who couldn't see except for the shadows of things. She says, *I'm not talking about literal sight.* But I am. I'm talking about literally being seen. Like the time before my daughter was born when my husband caught me dipping my finger into the toilet after I'd peed in it. I licked the finger clean. Thing is, I was told that that's one way to make sure you have a daughter. A neighbor told me that, the same neighbor who got caught shoplifting eggplants. Told her, *Eggplants aren't even good.* Anyway, I got a daughter, didn't I? A daughter who doesn't have to worry about her mother-in-law moving in like mine did. I swear, that woman cut holes in my clothes and pretended moths did it. I've never had moths. I kill those motherfuckers with my own bare hands. I clap them down like wannabe angels and crush with my heels their brittle haloes.

I once threw a pencil at a fly and pierced it through the heart, if flies even have hearts. My mother-in-law saw me and said that was my aborigine blood, that habit of skewering things alive. And another time she picked up all my dishes after I'd washed them and said they weren't clean enough. *They're clean enough to see your ugly face with,* I wanted to say. Almost told her, *Go eat out of your own ass, that's all your mouth is good for.* She tried to move into the bedroom with me and my husband. Said some fei hua about how her room down in the garage was too close to the kitchen, which has a microwave, which will kill her with its rays. Wanted to microwave her head until the brain-yolk dribbled hot from her ears. The first time my mother-in-law pretended to die, she staged a fall.

She went into the kitchen and wet the floor and threw all my plates to the ground. Those plates were what I brought here from the island all those years ago. Everyone told me not to take fragile things onto a plane, because they break. Something about air pressure or the sky's weight. But all the things I packed were breakable. I brought a glass ashtray that my mother once threw at my father's head. It hit him in the eye and now he can't see the meat of things. He can only see their shadows. So that he could see where my hands were, I had to shine a flashlight on them, cast their shape on a wall. I keep the ashtray to remind myself I have a shadow. Sometimes you can't tell what's a body or what's a shadow. For years I stepped around this big spot on the sidewalk I thought was water or piss or something. Turns out it was the shadow of a tree I hadn't looked up to see. I look at the ground more and more these days. Better to keep your eyes where your feet are.

Anyway, my mother-in-law lay down among all the things (mine!) she broke and pretended she'd fallen on the wet floor. Fallen doing what? The woman doesn't do anything but follow me around all day and tell me to take her to the dentist. Claims she's got teeth cancer, sometimes jaw cancer. Is there even such thing? For all I know, *I've* got jaw cancer. I ran to my mother-in-law and helped her up, but I could see there was no bruise on her. The only thing she'd done was bite her tongue a little, and it wasn't even bleeding. I'd give her my blood to bleed with, that's how generous I am, but she's never been hurt in her life. After that, she insisted on walking around the house using a broomstick as a cane. I've seen that woman jump three feet into the air to smack a mosquito with her hands. One night I saw her drop the cane and run to the TV so she could catch the opening scene of her soap opera, about an empress dowager controlling her puppet son. You see how fake?

Then the second time she tried, it was with a rope. She tried to hang herself in the pantry, except when I opened the door, her feet were still on the ground. Sure, the rope was around her neck and tied to the rafter and everything, but the pantry's only four and a half feet tall and she was just standing there, leashed to the ceiling. She even tried to pretend she was choking by sticking her tongue out and making these coughing sounds, but when I asked her what the hell she was doing, she paused to say, *I'm killing myself because you are a bad daughter-in-law and what will my son think when he finds out I've killed myself because of you how bad he will feel how much he will regret marrying you choosing you you bitch.* I said, *If you can say all that while hanging yourself, you're going to live.* And the third time was the worst. She stole the neighbor's kiddie pool and filled it up in the yard and pretended to drown in it. Except she didn't fill it up enough and there was only about a knuckle of water in there, and when she thrashed around, most of it splashed out of the pool and then she had to continue pretending to drown in nothing. She flopped facedown and tried to be dead, but the whole pool deflated from the weight of her body—let me tell you, she's got hips like hams— and as the air came out, it made a farting sound. Instead of dying, it sounded like she needed to shit. The fourth time was also a drowning, except this one was in the bathtub. I heard her filling it up and I was ready this time. As soon as she got into the tub with all her clothes on, I burst through the door, said, *Not while I'm alive,* and dragged her out by the hair. Turns out her hair is not very strongly attached to her scalp, so I ended up tearing out a lot of it, and she cried for almost a month about it, told my husband I was abusing her and now she'd have to wear a wig. I know ways to abuse her, and none of them involve her hair. I could heat up a frying pan and

press it to her face until the skin sizzles and all her features
melt together into an abstract painting. I could push her feet
into a pot of hot water and boil them till they rise like dumplings. I could scalp her and then wear her skin like a swim cap.

All my friends say what I'm dealing with is nothing: They
have mothers-in-law who have locked them inside the garage
on 105-degree days, that have put manure in their food and
claimed it was the recipe, as if they have ever used a recipe.
The worst thing is when some of them convert our children
into loving their nainais better than they love their own mothers. That's when you have to tell your daughters the truth of
everything that's been done to you, all the times you were told
you were a bad xífù for eating with your head bent over the
bowl, for shopping at Nordstrom Rack instead of going to
the temple, for overstuffing dumplings into testicle-looking
things. So what if I like them big. And then you tell your
daughter all the stories in history about mothers-in-law who
beat concubines to death with a chamber pot, mothers-in-law
who rip themselves open by shoving their sons' full-grown
heads back inside themselves, sometimes up the wrong hole, a
mother-in-law who wakes you up at three in the morning so
that you can drive her to the emergency room because, she
claims, she's pregnant at the age of seventy-seven and is having a baby right now, it's inside her, rolling around like a juiced
grapefruit, it's sour and screaming, and when you finally get
there, an hour later because she tells you there's a shortcut
even though the only direction she knows is toward the church,
it turns out she has kidney stones and you're going to have to
pay for their removal, out of pocket, and the rest is debt you'll
have for life, and when the doctor rolls her into surgery, you
tell him, *Please just let her die on the operating table,* or *Please
pretend to operate on her but leave the stones inside her, make*

*her feel the birth-pain of passing those blessed pebbles through
her body.*

But the doctor doesn't listen, he removes them and then
stitches her up and she loses basically no blood, and she goes
home the next day and tells you it's your fault for using too
much soy sauce in all your dishes, even though the reason you
add a spoonful more is that she told you in the first place that
nothing you make is salty enough. The fifth time she tries to
kill herself is when she walks out to the highway—without
her cane, of course—and steps in front of an 18-wheeler, except by some miracle, the 18-wheeler stops right before it hits
her and there's an eight-car pileup and we see her on the local
evening news. It's a physics-defying miracle, how an elderly
woman who is terribly neglected at home—because of course
she has to say that on TV—has been saved thanks to a truck-
er's quick reflexes and the benevolent will of god. She's being
called a saint in certain comments sections, and I might have
left a comment or two as well, all of them about how people
aren't really supposed to live forever, in other eras they would
be dead by seventy-seven, and being pulped by an 18-wheeler
is actually, I imagine, a very merciful end, and it probably
leaves a beautiful piece of blood-art on the highway, kind of
like a mural you can only see from above.

They even interview her for the *World Journal,* and of
course she tells the reporter she doesn't blame her daughter-
in-law for not taking better care of her, because how can a
woman like her, at her age, be valued in a world like this,
where old women are seen as burdens? But god had said otherwise; god had held back an 18-wheeler and said, *You are wor-
thy of my love and intervention.* I almost strangle her in her
bed after that. I stand over her in the dark and think about it,
just think about it. The sixth time, I tell my husband it's all his

fault. He should have been immaculately conceived by a goat.
Every man loves his mother milk-sour. I tell you, my husband
never once took my side. One time my mother-in-law told me
I'd overcooked the fish, but that fish was so soft inside it almost
dissolved in the light. And my husband said nothing to defend
me, even though he'd eaten half the fish himself, and my
daughter the lesbian only knows enough Chinese to say, *I don't
want, thank you.* Like a damn cricket, she says it again and
again. I want her to tell me my fish is done perfect. Look how
the bones disrobe. This woman tells me I can't cook a fish? I'll
cook her. Later she says she wants the master bedroom because
the garage is full of outside-air, and outside-air is full of toxins
that are souring her, can't you see how her neck sags, how her
breasts are hard as potatoes, how her tongue is purple? I want
to say, *Your neck sags because you're an old shit-sack, your
breasts are hard because you don't take them out to breathe, your
tongue is purple from that time you bit it instead of dying.*

I don't say anything about the fish, and I don't apologize
either, so that night she puts her head in the oven but forgets
to turn it on. I come downstairs in the morning and she is
asleep, drooling, with her head poked into the oven. I ask her
where she learned to do this oven thing and she says she's been
reading, even though I know that woman is illiterate. She's
one of those peasant women who's so short she looks like a
pack animal from afar, a body built to carry things. I'm a better mother to her son than she is. That's what marriage is,
motherhood, except the man doesn't do you the courtesy of
growing up. I tell her, *Next time just swallow the insecticide we
keep on the shelf in the garage.* She looks at me angry, because
I am supposed to say, *No, don't die, we need you, your son needs
you,* etc. I bend down really close to her face and say, *The oven
is electric.* Then I tell her, *The way gas works, you could have*

*killed everyone in this house. Is that what you want, to kill your
own son in his sleep?*

And that's when she stands up, a foot shorter than me. It's
morning and my daughter is waking up. I can hear her in the
next room, walking around without socks on even though I tell
her you can die that way. I like to be awake before she is. I'm
glad she won't have a man. Better not to be a mother. *It leads
to many suicides,* I should tell her. My mother-in-law starts
telling me this story about how she didn't know she was pregnant. The night her son was born, she thought she was having
gas. She was alone. But then my husband slipped out of her
like a fish and everyone said, *Kill it.* That's when she left for
the island, the baby dragged behind her in a net. I call her a
liar. I won't forget the time she caught my husband washing a
dish and called my own mother in Yilan to complain how I
wasn't doing my duty as a wife, how I made her son clean in
his own home, how I threatened him with a back scratcher
into rinsing that dish, and of course my mother believed this
and called to tell me I would never grow skin, as if, as if my
husband has ever washed a dish, as if he's ever washed anything but his own dick, and even that not very well.

The problem is this, I tell my daughter: Mothers grow up
married to their sons, but we're born knowing our daughters
will leave us. Not because we want them to, but because we
never had them, not really: They belong to the men we give
them to. Men, they belong to everything, including themselves. This is what I say: We should separate all mothers and
sons at birth and grow them in different dirts. Make the sons
grow up alone. And mothers, we'll be fine in our own rooms.
Give us a window or two, a view, curtains that open into morning. All those times she almost killed herself, she didn't know
death isn't like a man: It won't just take you anytime you're on

your back. When she finally dies, I won't pretend I'm not happy about it. But I'll buy her a good burial, a full funeral. I'll give her an urn with a name on it, which is more than her family would have done, her family who doesn't even name their daughters. That woman answers to nothing. I can't even pray her dead, because the gods don't have her listed in any directory. When my husband dies, I'll bury him beneath her. And I won't mourn then either. You can have his bones and the moths they'll become. I joke now with my daughter, not that it matters to her, since the only men she'll marry are women, and two women together probably cancel out, become nameless. I point at the sky. *The sun*, I say, and laugh. When choosing a sun to see by, make sure it's got no mother. The moon, that's the mother. Her eye is always open to watch her sun. *It's not really a light,* my daughter says about the moon, *it's a mirror.* But mirrors, I tell her, are more dangerous than anything. A mirror's only meaning is to multiply. To duplicate. To duty. The mirror doesn't change what is shown to it, not unless someone shatters the glass, and that would be you, my daughter, the fist to my ribs, the one who will never become the moon.

Mandarin Speakers

When the aliens come, they will speak Chinese. Abu says it's because one in five people speak Chinese. It's strategic for us to pray in Mandarin, maximizing the number of ghosts and/or gods who will deliver us justice. One in five dead people are Chinese, most likely. Abu loves statistics and reads them aloud to me every morning before her job at the button factory: For example, the average American generates nearly 4.5 pounds of trash each day. Unintentional drowning is the third-leading cause of injury death, according to 2016. *What about intentional drowning?* I ask this, but Abu says don't talk about that. Americans are so wasteful, Abu says. I was born 4.5 pounds, the same size as an average American's one-day waste. When I was born, my spine lifted itself through the skin like a mast, and Abu had to stitch it flat. I was so small, my aunts cradled me inside a rice bowl. I slept with the dishes and didn't outgrow a fork till I was a year old. After reading the statistic about American garbage, Abu doesn't let us throw away anything—no flushing toilet paper, because our pipes are weak as the neighbor's throat, which stalls unless it's singing. She sings every night when the Sichuan opera's on TV, her face painted thick as a scab. Paper towels are sinful: Only towels and old T-shirts can eat our stains. Even the hair our pillows are hoarding can be used for something: Abu makes dolls out of the hair we coax from the drain-throat and harvest from our beds. The fish bones we don't throw away either, reusing them instead as transparent toothpicks, plucking up cubes of papaya that look like they're levitating from our fingers.

Abu says we will reject American wastefulness, that everything has a purpose, but she keeps a collection of wiped tapes with Teresa Teng's faded face on them, and she keeps my baby teeth strung on a necklace, and she keeps a leather-banded Seiko watch that's always ahead of us, and she keeps the syringes used to inject Ama's insulin even though Ama is ash now and I never knew her, and in heaven Ama will definitely not understand our prayers in Mandarin because she only ever spoke Taiwanese, siau gin na, *you crazy crab girl* is what she would have called me, and Abu says Taiwanese is toneless, overhead like bad weather, nothing like the way Mandarin sounds when the TV people speak it, naming wars and husbands and storms, their tongues tallying up casualties, their teeth electrified into a fence. No use knowing a language no one will listen to, Abu says: You might as well speak for shadows. She's learning Mandarin offscreen, staying up all night to watch soap operas where the actresses get hit by cars and develop amnesia, unable to remember the men they love, and I ask her if that's why Baba's not here, because she got hit by a car and forgot him. Abu sucks on red melon seeds, spits the shells into the conch of my palm. *No*, Abu says, *I remember everything. That's worse.*

My problem, besides being born 4.5 pounds, is that I still throw things away. When Abu is away at the factory, when my aunts are asleep or tailoring jeans in the living room, where the ceiling is constellated with leaks, or when they're meeting men with mouths like guillotines, severing every sentence that is spoken to them, I scratch Teresa Teng's face off the tapes with my thumbnails, blow the flakes onto the street. I seduce the ants into tissues soaked in sugarwater and then throw them into the dumpster behind the dim sum restaurant. I poke the insulin needles into my thigh and inject breath into my arteries, then toss them spent into the gutters. I tug the neighbor's voice in through the window and ball it in my fists, discarding it out another window. We only have two windows, but they dislike each other. Whatever weather the bedroom window shows, the window in the living room has to contradict it. If it's raining in one window, the other window is sunbuzzed. If it's morning in this one, the night is mooning us in the other window. I live between the two, waiting for Abu to come home, and when she does, she asks me if I've made any waste today. No, I say, and then as proof I save all my used toilet paper in a plastic bag she will burn in the backyard when it's night and no one can call the cops on us for committing arson on the contents of our own bodies. Abu says burning something is not the same as throwing it away: It's not the same as a landfill, not like sending something away to be forgotten. Fire is a form of memory, she says: Smoke is what survives after loss, what is inhaled by the sky and recycled into night.

Memory loss must be a symptom of Mandarin. That's what I learned from TV and all the women with amnesia, all the women who walk onto streets without looking. *Does that count as intentional death?* I say, and Abu says no one is hurt on TV.

It's all pretend, like when the neighbor cries on the phone for her husband to come home: She's performing for us, mimicking all the operas she loves, or how all the cars that drive onto our dead-end street turn around and rev away like we don't deserve the windows we're seen through, even though we recognize some of their faces through the windshield, all the daughters fluent in U-turn, looping their own lives, rhyming their futures with forgetting.

Someday, I say to Abu, *I will pray for you.* Abu says, *Pray in Mandarin, and I'll learn to understand you.* But I hoard the Taiwanese words she says unintentionally, always unintentionally, like when her thumb grazes the stove and she says, *Jia sai,* or when the TV actress who forgets her family name is taken home from the hospital in a brand-new car that's quiet as a watermelon seed and Abu says that's ho giah lang for you, or when I'm asleep at night and she leans above me, mouth leaky as the ceiling, and says, *Don't forget me, don't forget me, baitok, baitok, baitok.*

One time, Abu comes home with a plastic bottle full of buttons. She keeps all our plastic bottles and rinses and reuses them so many times that the plastic is thin as skin and flinches when you touch it. She says, *This is an instrument,* and shakes the bottleful of buttons while she shimmies through the kitchen, flicking a chopstick against the refrigerator door, the edge of the sink, my forehead, a rhythm I remember to. The buttons are every color of the weather, blues and grays and blacks, and I want to arrange them on the ceiling in constellations. I want to unbutton the stars with my fingers and forget them inside my fist. When stars aren't on fire, they must look like buttons sewn flat against the sky, waiting to be undone. I arrange the buttons on my mattress and flick them into the air, teaching them to UFO. I bring them to the sink full of dishwater and drown them one by one, but some of them are hollow and gold and bob up when I drop them, and so I tally their survival rate and invent my own statistic: Drowning is the number-one cause of floating. Abu sees me playing and says she hates buttons because she has to make them. I ask her if she hates me because she had to make me. No, she says, and laughs at the buttons I suck shiny, the way I toss them over my shoulder like coins and make a wish before they land: for the aliens to land on our roof and say we've been listening to your prayers without needing subtitles, we've been fluent in you forever. I lay the buttons on my cheekbones, each as warm as a mole on Abu's face, and I will never throw them away. Abu says buttons are for doing and undoing, but she will never undo me, though long ago she considered it, considered unmaking me because she was husbandless and motherless, considered ripping me out like a stitch, but that was a long time ago, before I accumulated inside her like 4.5 pounds of an average American's waste, before I taught her the Mandarin word for pray, for god, for give, forgive the weight I became in her palms that day, every day she didn't throw me away.

Anchor

When Second Aunt Huilin was ten, she learned how to assemble a gun and fire it. There was a class called Invasion at her elementary school. In the wetlands outside, where the mud climbed your spine, the teacher demonstrated how to take aim and fire straight. The children worked with blanks first, aiming at where the top of the cane field slit open the sky like a wrist. Then they used real bullets, shooting soldiers made of leaf-stuffed sacks and watermelons for heads. The teacher said to shoot from somewhere low, on your belly or from a trench, just in case the enemy fired back. Aunt Huilin shot while squatting. A few sack-soldiers were lined up in front of the cane field, and the others were hidden among the cane stalks to simulate a real ambush. You got a prize if your bullet burst a watermelon, meat flying like shrapnel and embedding into the sky. You got to scour the fields first and eat all the best chunks, the ones without seeds, the sweetest bits of the soldier's brain. As the second-best shot in class, Aunt Hui-

lin went home every night with her belly the size of a melon,
big enough to rebirth what she'd eaten.

One day when they were firing into the cane field, Aunt
Huilin's bullet hit a real body. She said she felt it immediately:
After a month of shooting, the bullets she fired were as sen-
tient as her fingertips, and she could feel the air parting around
them and stitching itself whole again. Her bullet hit a girl
playing in the cane field. It wasn't harvest season yet, and the
cane in some parts of the field was stubbly as a beard. In the
thick of the field, where the soldiers were planted, someone's
daughter had wandered in and sat there all morning.

They stopped firing. The air turned to fur, stroking their
faces with smoke. Aunt Huilin dropped her pistol and the
teacher waded into the cane, dragging the girl out of the field
by her feet. The girl was actually a baby, about the same size as
two watermelons balanced on the sacks. No one knew her
name, and no one came to claim her. What Aunt Huilin remembers is that her face was intact everywhere except for her
mouth, which had been torn out of her face with a force that
seemed impossible. Her mouth was a hole, and not in the way
that all mouths were holes: You could see the sky coming
through the girl's face. You could peer right through the wound
like a window.

Aunt Huilin would conclude the story by saying all those
bullets were sponsored by American military money, which
her niece Sylvia thought was a cheap ending: a way to pluck
herself clean out of the story, a way to sever herself from the
ending. Aunt Huilin always told this story with a pair of scissors in her hands, snipping at the end of every sentence, ex-
perimenting with the length of her dyed-red bob. She
managed a hair-and-nail salon in the Pacific Rim strip mall

and cut hair for all the women in the neighborhood, keeping rolls of cash tips in duct-taped margarine tubs.

Sylvia always wanted to know more about the girl's face, but her aunt would only turn away and say that after the girl was shot, they still had to walk through the field and eat every shard of watermelon off the ground, even the pieces that steamed with blood. Nothing edible should ever be edited out.

She told Sylvia the story again when they were outside the Salvation Army, parking in the spot farthest from the entrance and nearest to a dumpster. *I'm not going in*, Aunt Huilin said. Sylvia told her aunt that the Salvation Army wasn't technically fighting anything, wasn't technically anybody's army, but she knew her aunt wouldn't believe it.

It's not an army, and there are books in there, Sylvia said, books with spines tagged with pink stickers that meant they were only a dime. She knew Aunt Huilin read romance novels exclusively, all of them starring blond men with green eyes who rode horses and wielded swords. For her whole childhood, Sylvia assumed the romance was between the man and the horse, until her aunt informed her that that was sick.

Sylvia drove her aunt home and said they could turn around at any time and return to the Salvation Army store. But her aunt opened the window and stuck her head out to say no, as if Sylvia were located somewhere in the sky. Sylvia didn't want to buy anything at the Salvation Army store they hadn't already owned before: Her aunt had donated all of Baiyang's things to the temple, and when Sylvia called to ask, the temple said they'd donated everything to the Salvation Army. Sylvia only wanted to buy his things back, to populate Baiyang's room like a museum of reclaimed artifacts. She'd wanted her aunt to walk into the store and see his belongings like mounted carcasses and regret ever giving them a grave.

When they got home, Baiyang's room was the temperature of a meat locker, and Sylvia suspected that her aunt had tampered with the air inside it. When Aunt Huilin went downstairs to watch the island news on TV, Sylvia turned on the lights in the room she shared with Baiyang—Aunt Huilin's only son, her only cousin—and looked down at the empty socket of the bedframe. Even the mattress had been donated. She and Baiyang had shared the mattress since they were little, and there was still a stain on the right side from the first time Sylvia got her period. Aunt Huilin had run into the room when Sylvia yelled, looking down at the blood and then at her own hands as if she'd shot Sylvia herself.

Sylvia sat cross-legged in the center of the bedframe, the empty boards bouncing her up and down like a trampoline. The ceiling was wrinkled with leaks, some as long as her palms, others that rivered across the whole length of the ceiling diagonally. They mapped out a continent she and Baiyang couldn't ever read, and whenever it rained at night while they were in bed, the water fingered out of the cracks and lunged for their lips. Aunt Huilin had sealed the leaks with variations of duct tape, caulk, and Silly Putty, but the water charged through the ceiling anyway, and Baiyang and Sylvia held on to the sides of the bedframe like a boat big enough for just their bodies.

Baiyang liked to say that he was the boat and Sylvia was the anchor: Years ago, Aunt Huilin and Sylvia's mother planned to come to California together. Baiyang started crowning while Aunt Huilin was in the bathroom of the airplane, and because the plane hadn't taken off yet, he was technically born there and Sylvia was born here. Sylvia always joked that

Baiyang was ejected headfirst into the toilet, his body ringing the tin bowl like a bell.

In a hospital in California, Sylvia recoiled like a fist inside her mother's belly. *Your mother couldn't shit for months after you were born*, Aunt Huilin said. Aunt Huilin claimed that when her sister died a few years later, it wasn't because of the birth, but Sylvia always thought differently. Sylvia knew she'd opened her mother too fast. Bodies were like umbrellas, and if they were opened too far and too quickly, they flipped inside out and would never fold up correctly again.

Above the kitchen sink, Aunt Huilin hung a photo of her sister standing on a mud road in her Japanese-style school uniform, the mountains above her like an awning, the edges of the sky worn petal-thin. Once, Sylvia took down that photo to keep in her bedroom, and her aunt chased her and wrestled it away, stowing it in her own room. It made Sylvia angry, the way her aunt seemed to own all memories of her mother. She stole it again that night and took it with her to the bath, folding the photo into a boat and floating her mother on the surface, towing her across the water until she sank into sludge at the bottom of the tub.

Sylvia got up from the empty bedframe and opened Baiyang's closet, which was half hers. He'd taken almost nothing to the island, just two sets of shirts and one pair of pants, though they'd probably confiscate his belongings and stitch him into a uniform. He'd wanted to bring his toy foam-pellet pistol too, but Sylvia said, *You're about to spend a whole year with real, actual guns.* He said those weren't the same as this one. His gun wasn't trying to be real, which is why he liked it. The pistol was painted neon orange and shot foam bullets the size and shape of fingers. Their jellied tips stuck to the ceiling and wouldn't loosen for weeks. There was one in the kitchen, dangling from the ceiling like an udder, which neither Sylvia nor Baiyang remembered shooting.

When Sylvia went downstairs, her aunt was watching island news, reclined on the sofa with her legs splayed. The screen showed a black-and-white montage of boys doing military exercises, marching in lines, their grayed-out uniforms making them look like rain clouds, bloated and blurry, carrying more than their bodies. A reporter was interviewing bystanders at a rally protesting mandatory military service. *There's no use,* said someone's grandfather. *We might as well lie down on our backs and play dead.*

Aunt Huilin shut the TV off and stood up from the sofa. She always said if our home was broken into, we should platter ourselves and play dead, foam a bit at the mouth. The way to win, she told us, is to live. *Tomorrow we're going to go light incense for my son,* Aunt Huilin said. Sylvia didn't like the way she said *my son,* as if Baiyang were hers alone, as if he was not Sylvia's cousin-brother, as if the two of them hadn't spent the last day together before he left, shooting at a tree trunk with his foam-pellet gun. Sylvia turned the pistol on him and fired at his head. It landed on his forehead and horned him, as natural as if it'd grown out from between his eyes. *This is a test,* Sylvia said, and he'd failed. He hadn't ducked. Baiyang laughed and said, *But I knew it wasn't real.*

Sylvia told her aunt not to light incense for him like he was dead. *He's just away,* she said, *getting muddy in some field, probably.* Then she remembered how her aunt had shot the girl in the field and said nothing else. Aunt Huilin only repeated herself. *Don't go, don't go. Don't go,* she told her son for months before he left. *You have a choice,* she said, *always.* But Baiyang said he wanted to go. He said it was only going to be a year, and it was either go now or go when he was older and had responsibilities. My aunt said, *You have a responsibility right now, you have a responsibility to stay,* and Baiyang told her it wasn't true, pointing at Sylvia: *You're the anchor and I'm the vessel.* He had been born on an airplane, and some part of Sylvia believed that Baiyang never landed anywhere. *There's no war,* Baiyang said. *Don't worry about me.*

That's when Aunt Huilin first started talking about the cane field and the girl she killed, looping the same story until its end was knotted to the beginning, the girl's mouth becoming the gun's. Aunt Huilin said she didn't like anyone in a uniform, didn't like the curfew enforced when she was a girl: Once, she was beaten with the butt of a gun for walking home late. *Look,* she said, lifting her shirt, showing them the shadow that spread out from her spine and wrapped her ribs, the ghost of a bruise. Baiyang said this story was dogshit: He placed his palm on her back and pushed, saying, *It's not a real bruise; it's just a birthmark. You don't even flinch. You were born with this.* But Sylvia wasn't so sure: When her aunt rolled the hem of her shirt back down, it stuck to her back as if with blood.

Aunt Huilin said if Baiyang left, she'd donate everything he owned. He would come back to the house empty. *I can buy new things,* he said. *But you'll never get the same things back,* Aunt Huilin said. They were sitting at the dinner table and Sylvia was washing the dishes, forgetting the soap and wondering why they still weren't clean.

A month ago, while Baiyang was rinsing the dishes and Sylvia was drying, their faces merging together in reflection, he said he'd gotten his military-service letter. They were both commuter students at the community college down the street, but Baiyang told the school he was leaving. Sylvia scrubbed the plate harder, imagining it was stained with watermelon juice, so sticky that her hands were webbed with it. That night,

Aunt Huilin came home complaining that her hands smelled of feet, that a man had come in with some kind of fungus, dyeing his nails all kinds of stained-glass colors. Baiyang told her he was leaving, and Aunt Huilin pretended she hadn't heard him. She kept talking about the man's feet and how the soles were scarred with diagonal lines from the arch to the heel, the scars so deep that she lost her fingers inside them. *How do you even scar the soles of your feet?* she asked, and Baiyang answered by saying he was leaving.

That night, Sylvia fell asleep looking at the back of Baiyang's neck, wondering when he'd gotten that scar on his nape shaped like a hook, when he'd stopped sharing his dreams with her, always about water, always about floating belly-up in a giant porcelain toilet. They woke up side by side in the shipwreck of their room, the drawers missing from the armoire, their clothes fluttered open and scattered like flags on the floor, Baiyang's mirror taken down from the back of the door. When they got up, Sylvia realized that even Baiyang's pillow was gone, that he'd been sleeping on his forearm all night and now there was a bruise on the inside of his elbow.

Downstairs, Aunt Huilin was wearing a face mask like an exterminator, two black garbage bags swinging from her arms. She accused Sylvia of encouraging him to leave, but Sylvia said she hadn't, and it was the truth: She didn't know he was planning on going so soon, and besides, it was only going to be a year, not forever. The garbage bag hanging from her aunt's left arm tore open at the bottom, and Baiyang's clothing bled out onto the floor. She went into the kitchen, dragging both bags as if one hadn't broken, and Sylvia saw that all the kitchen drawers were flung open like jaws.

I should take your things too, she said to Sylvia, leaning both garbage bags against the pantry door. The face mask hid the shape of her mouth as she spoke, and her words sounded like they were coming from another body. *I should sell your things and pay off your debt.* Sylvia knew this meant her mother's debt to the hospital for the cost of her birth and its injuries, the bill her aunt had co-signed and inherited. Every year on Sylvia's birthday, her aunt claimed the debt was growing alongside Sylvia, and so she imagined it inside her own body: a hole in her stomach dilating wide enough that the sky would someday be stuffed into it.

Sylvia said again that Baiyang didn't have a choice, and even if he did, she didn't have anything to do with it. That morning, Baiyang watched Aunt Huilin slip his shoes into the garbage bag and said, *Fine, I'll go naked,* claiming he'd leave as soon as he could. By the time he left, Sylvia and Baiyang were sleeping every night on an empty bedframe, and Baiyang was wearing the same black shirt every day. The night Sylvia dropped him off at the airport, her aunt refused to come. Baiyang said he couldn't find his foam-pellet gun, the one he used to aim at the sky, pretending to be Hou Yi the warrior, who shot down the nine suns to save everyone from burning. Sylvia said she hadn't seen it. She remembered when he first brought it home from school that day in elementary school, saying it was a gift, when she knew he'd probably stolen it from some other kid. Aunt Huilin had taken it from his hands and tried to throw it away, but Baiyang started crying and gnawing his pinky, which he did whenever he wanted something: As soon as his teeth breached skin, Aunt Huilin would dislodge the finger from his mouth and touch it to her own lips. *My son,* she always called him in front of Sylvia, never *your cousin* or *your brother,* as if it to remind Sylvia who he belonged to and who Sylvia didn't.

It was night when Baiyang's plane took off, and Sylvia

wondered whether he'd use the bathroom and try to recall his own birth: Aunt Huilin bracing herself over the toilet, praying it was only a bowel movement. If she could hold him in for a day longer, he'd surface in another country.

The day after Sylvia and Aunt Huilin argued outside the Salvation Army, Sylvia drove her aunt from the salon to the temple in Milpitas, parking in the overheated lot where the buckets of ash were emptied out. The temple was a repurposed rec center, beige plaster on the outside and frayed red carpeting on the inside, a Buddha statue at the front of the room that looked like it was spray-painted gold. Its arms were shedding paint, and the skin beneath was blue.

Before they'd left for temple, Sylvia received an email from Baiyang—he promised he'd find a way to write to her, even if he had to saddle a flock of birds with his words. Sylvia said it would be impossible, since he wouldn't have Wi-Fi or cell service, but she should have known: Everything was possible for him, especially leaving. The email said, *There are fucking monkeys everywhere.* She wasn't sure if he meant the monkeys themselves were fucking. She tried to imagine Baiyang's face varnished with oil and greasepaint and mud, climbing a tree with bare hands and feet or steering a tank through a field, but all she could imagine was Baiyang saying, *What you're imagining isn't real. Only on TV.*

It was a joke between them: *only on TV.* Until they were twelve, Sylvia and Baiyang had never seen a white person except on TV. For years they thought that all white people were actors. *How terrible,* they said, to be born to play someone else, to never be your own body. They thought it was sad to live onscreen like that, never known by your own name. There were a few in their seventh-grade class, but Sylvia assumed they were just rehearsing for their future roles, practicing the characters they'd soon appear as.

Sylvia and her aunt entered the temple and nodded at the names of the dead flagging the walls. There was a foldout card table in the corner with molasses cookies so stale they'd nick your teeth, pink shrimp chips that looked like packing peanuts, and a pot of tea with no cups to drink out of.

They knelt in front of the paint-flaked Buddha, touching their foreheads to the red pleather cushion before rising. They lit incense and screwed the sticks into the sandy pit to the left of the Buddha. Sylvia prayed for Baiyang to send longer emails, for her debt to pay itself so that her aunt could retire, and, most of all, for her to get her own mattress back, because sleeping on an empty bedframe was starting to make her spine sour.

When they were finished, Sylvia stood by the foldout table while her aunt chanted from a book Sylvia couldn't read, the characters lined up neat as soldiers. There was a new nun ringing the bell in the corner, her head not yet shaved like the others. Under her orange robes, she wore a pair of suede cowboy boots. She lifted the hem of her robe to clean a pair of wire-framed glasses that had to be nudged up her nose every time she swung the rope, ringing the bell with so much force the air vibrated as visibly as water. When the nun let go, Sylvia watched her wipe her hands on her robes, erasing the sweat from her palms. She had never thought nuns were capable of sweating: They always entered the temple in two rows, their hands cupped in front of their bodies, eyes pinned precisely to the back of each other's heads, soundless and never sweaty.

The nun saw Sylvia looking and took up the rope again, though it wasn't time to ring the bell. Then she dropped it

again, the knotted end of the rope swinging like an animal's
tail. She walked toward Sylvia with her eyes down, and when
she lifted them, Sylvia saw that the nun's pupils were slightly
blued, a sheen that reminded her of a crow's underwing.

The nun asked her why she'd come today, her voice low
enough that Sylvia had to lean toward her. The collar of her
robe was a shade darker with sweat. Sylvia said she was praying for her brother. It was easier to say *brother*. The nun asked
if he'd passed away, and Sylvia said *never*, then *not yet*. He was
just serving his mandatory military service, Sylvia said, but
there wasn't a war. The nun nodded, her glasses sliding down
her nose. Sylvia wanted to reach up and take them off her face,
but she knew it was an unholy thing to do.

When the nun asked why Sylvia was praying for him, Sylvia turned to her aunt, who was still folded over her book,
mowing rows of words with her finger. She said, *There's a
debt, too, that I still need to pay back. Not a spiritual debt*, Sylvia
said. *A real one. I mean, a money one.* The nun nodded again.
This time, when her glasses slipped, she caught them in her
hand and slid them into her robes. She asked Sylvia to take a
walk with her around the perimeter of the temple, where she
said her blessings, and they would discuss how to settle her
debts.

They circled the parking lot first, and when the nun bent
her head to pray, Sylvia said the only holy word she knew:
Amituofo. She wondered if she was allowed to ask the nun's
name, or if the nun even still had one. Sylvia wanted to ask
when her head was going to be shaved: Her hair was longer
than Sylvia's, down to her elbows, and strands of it floated in
the air like smoke. Sylvia mourned it already. If she reached
up and touched the floating pieces, she thought, maybe they
would dissolve. If she leaned close enough to the nun's neck,

maybe she could inhale the nun's hair straight out of the air. Sylvia wondered if it was right to be thinking about touching a nun and then decided she would never ask.

The nun asked what the debt was, and Sylvia said it was the kind that kept swallowing her. When the nun nodded and said nothing, Sylvia said, *I don't know how to pray to something without a body.* When they were finished walking around the temple three times, the nun turned around and perched her right hand on Sylvia's shoulder. It was a touch so sudden that Sylvia almost ducked to kneel on the pavement before her. The nun looked at her with unfocused eyes, and Sylvia realized that when she wasn't wearing glasses, every face was as vague as a landscape. Sylvia felt comforted by this, as if they were speaking with a country between them. The nun said she had a story to tell and that, after this story, Sylvia would need to pray again.

The story was this: When she was little and not yet a nun, she lived alone with her mother, who told her about a girl living by the sea. Back then, the beach was staked with broken glass bottles to defend against an invasion, so she never got to play on the shore. One day the girl saw a whale in the water. It opened its mouth and inside was a couch, a TV, a high-rise apartment, everything the girl ever wanted, but to enter the water she had to run through the field of bottle-glass stakes. Because she knew skin would grow back, she ran until her soles were ribboned and all the bones of her feet bared themselves. She swam into the whale's mouth and disappeared.

That sounds biblical, Sylvia said. *Aren't you supposed to be Buddhist?* The girl laughed and said the story wasn't about the whale, it was about want. Sylvia swallowed, not remembering when she'd started thinking of the nun as just a girl.

That's not the end of the story either, the girl said. *She lived inside the whale for many years. There was Wi-Fi inside it. She threw her trash out its shithole. She lived in the sea so deep there was never any news of war. Then one day the whale motorized, flew out of the water, and became a China Airlines flight and landed in America and deposited the girl. She was in Los Angeles. She was alone. No money but a whale's tooth. She asked the water why the whale had abandoned her, but she was not really abandoned. She was paying back her debt in exile. She had not been living in the whale for free. All those years she was living under the sea, not hearing, free of paying anything, she had been accruing a karmic debt and now it was dealt.*

Sylvia told the nun this was a dogshit story. That the girl hadn't done anything in the first place but want something, and didn't we all desire? *And don't you want anything too?* Sylvia asked, but she already knew: By severing her hair soon, the nun-girl would be swearing not to. She looked at her and squinted, and Sylvia couldn't tell if the nun-girl didn't believe her or if she was trying to see Sylvia's face clearer. *Everything has a debt,* the nun-girl said. *Every death is a payment.* After Aunt Huilin shot the girl in the cane field, everyone in town said that the killer would someday pay it off with her own daughter's life. But Sylvia knew the killer didn't have a daughter; she only had Baiyang, who she could no longer keep from wandering.

Sylvia walked away from the story, back into the temple, where someone was celebrating the hundredth day of death. A name was untacked from the wall and burned in a bucket, ashes rasping in the air. Aunt Huilin was still kneeling on her cushion, facing Buddha's draped hand, and the way she spoke with her mouth barely opening—as if she were underwater and afraid to drown—reminded Sylvia that her aunt's debt was deeper than her own.

Sylvia had spent many hours circling the hospital where she was born and where her mother bled for many hours. There was a story she once read about a pregnant woman who refused to give birth and barricaded herself in a hospital room, then attempted to break out through a window. Sylvia imagined that one of the shards punctured her belly, forcing her to give birth to a bellyful of steam.

Sylvia liked to thread in and out the hospital's parking lot and pretend to be waiting for a patient. Baiyang had laughed and said she was the only one whose ritual was a form of punishment, but Sylvia didn't consider it a punishment. There was an apartment building across from the hospital, and in the parking lot in front of it, a group of boys kicked a soccer ball against a fence. Every time they kicked, the wood fence flinched to avoid impact. The kids' mothers were sitting on foldout chairs, smoking the same kind of cigarettes Aunt Huilin hid between the cushions of the sofa. The mothers were watching their sons, and Sylvia could tell which boy belonged to which woman by the way his mother gazed at him with the precision of a weapon. The only thing her aunt ever told her about her mother was that she was the best shot in the entire fifth-grade class. *She never missed. She never hit anything she wasn't aiming at. She could hit a bird in the beak, a watermelon in the seed.* Sylvia watched those mothers, their tank tops streaked with sweat, and wondered which one was looking for her. She looked for a woman with hands that could span a sky. Her mother as a girl, white bucket hat, navy school uniform, eating watermelon meat and riddling the mud with seeds, spitting, teaching her sister how to train her hands steady by plunging them into a bucket of water and making no rings. *If I can see the surface move, I know it's you. Don't shake. Still the water in your fists.*

One of the boys kicked the soccer ball into the side of the apartment building, puncturing the plaster, and all the other boys ran forward, reaching their hands into the hole, birthing the ball out of the dark, lifting it alive.

Sylvia and her aunt left the temple, and the nun-girl was still standing outside by the doorway, watching them as they pulled out of the lot. When Sylvia had passed through the doorway, the nun-girl said to her only: *Come back soon.* In the car, Sylvia asked her aunt if she knew who the new nun was and if her head was going to be shaved soon. She missed it already: the nun-girl's hair swinging in time to the bell she rang. Aunt Huilin said she didn't know.

There was a new email from Baiyang by the time Sylvia was home: *With my hair cut I have mosquito bites all over my scalp when I itch in my sleep they bleed. On my face too now I'm red like those monkeys everywhere.* Sylvia emailed back, asking what breed of monkey lived there, but his response was a photo of mud. In the mud was a drawing of himself: Baiyang leaning against a tank made of leaves. His head looked too large for his body, his neck a wilted stem. Reaching up in the dark, Sylvia felt for the shape of her skull beneath her own hair and thought that watermelons were inaccurate: A real man's head was much smaller, much harder to hit. When Sylvia looked at his arms, two twigs in the mud, she almost expected to see him holding a toy gun.

Her aunt returned to watching the TV. While the screen replayed satellite footage of someone's sea, Sylvia called the Salvation Army store and asked if they'd recently received a toy gun. The woman on the phone said the store didn't accept toy guns anymore because someone had complained: Certain toys could expose young children to violence. Sylvia hung up. When it was night, her aunt was still surveilling the TV, as if the screen would shudder and unleash the sea behind it, carrying them both to Baiyang. Sylvia said it was time to go to bed. She had school tomorrow and her aunt had work. Aunt Huilin said, *No, it's still daytime on the island.* She was holding some kind of vigil, wanting to be awake when Baiyang was awake, even though Sylvia kept saying Baiyang wouldn't know the difference.

Sylvia slept on the bedframe with her hands behind her head, the leaks in the ceiling spitting water even though it wasn't raining. She imagined that the roof was backlogged with rain and someday the whole ceiling would surrender.

When she woke in the dark, her shirt was salt-stiff and heavy with sweat. The cracks in the ceiling looked wide as riverbeds. She'd had a dream about red-faced monkeys who ate the hair off her head, scraping back the skin of her scalp and rapping on the back like a melon, sniffing for the meat inside. When Sylvia sat up, the boards of the bedframe flexed beneath her and there was a girl in the doorway. The girl was so small that Sylvia thought at first it was an animal on all fours, but she had two legs, both folded beneath her, and her face was missing its lower half. Her jawbone was there, bare and glowing like milk, but her mouth was meatless. She wore pants only, the fabric stained at the crotch, the hem uneven as teeth.

When the girl didn't move, Sylvia got up from the bed and walked on her knees toward the doorway. *You don't know my name and I don't know yours,* Sylvia said, *but maybe we're related.* The girl was still, and when Sylvia came close enough, she looked through the hole in the girl's face. The night threaded through her head, a wrist-thick river. When Sylvia moved her eyes away from the hole, the girl twisted her torso and crawled toward the hallway. Sylvia tried to follow, but the girl's body frayed into shadow, a dark shape on the wall that spidered up toward the ceiling.

Sylvia went back to bed, but even when she closed her eyes, the hole in the girl's face hovered above, dilating the leaks in the ceiling. In the morning, while her aunt was at work, Sylvia took the bus to the temple, passing the landfill that smelled ripe and sweet, the sun a fruit bashed open for the flies. At the temple, the morning prayers were just beginning, and from the parking lot, Sylvia could hear the blood-hum of voices rising above the building. Sylvia was standing outside the gray doors, wondering whether she could enter in the middle of prayer, when the nun-girl approached from the side of the building. She'd been circling and praying, blessing the perimeter, and now she reached forward and offered a cupped hand as if wanting Sylvia to drink from it.

Before Sylvia left for the temple, she'd sent Baiyang an email: *Saw a gui,* she wrote. Then added: *maybe.* Then she deleted it all and rewrote: *Saw the girl with her mouth gone. Ghost?*

The nun-girl said the service was starting and would end in four hours. She said Sylvia could join if she wanted, but Sylvia shook her head and said, *I came to see you.* If she ever told her aunt about the ghost, Aunt Huilin would convert the entire house to smoke or at least light a fire in the doorway, and Sylvia would be commanded to jump over, leaving the ghosts behind on the other side. But Sylvia didn't want to scour the ghost from her house: She wanted the girl to speak, even if she had no mouth.

Sylvia told the nun-girl that she was being followed. The nun-girl nodded, her hair hitched to the air, suspended by some kind of static. *Because of the debt,* the nun-girl said, and Sylvia said she already knew that. *If you already know,* the nun-girl said, *then why aren't you paying it?* Sylvia wanted to say she'd already paid it, paid it with her mother, but instead she said, *I just wanted to see you at the temple again, to make sure your hair was still long.* The nun-girl turned to the side, her hand reaching up to touch the nape of her neck beneath her hair, and Sylvia resisted reaching forward to touch the tip of the nun-girl's eyelashes. When Sylvia said she would go home and pray now, the nun-girl lowered her chin and went back to blessing the building, her palms cupped and lifted as if she were searching for a leak.

At home, Sylvia checked her phone and saw that Baiyang had replied, though it was too late for him to be awake: He'd sent her another blurred photo, this time of a monkey. She thought the monkey was red-furred all over, but when she looked closer, she saw that its belly had been split open, its face a cracked garnet. It had been run over by something or dropped from a height, though she didn't think it was possible for a monkey to fall. Then she read the caption: *Someone got bored.*

That night in bed, Sylvia pretended again that the bedframe was a boat, and it was the first time she steered it alone. Usually, Baiyang sat by the headboard and pretended to captain the bed, extending an arm ahead of him whenever he sighted land. Sylvia played the anchor, and when they neared whatever shore Baiyang claimed to see, she stiffened her body and rolled off the edge of the bed.

Sylvia sat cross-legged in the center of the bedframe and rowed through the air until her arms felt like splintering. Near morning, the mouthless girl crawled into the doorway, and her jawbone had yellowed since the night before. There was a gun lying flat in her palms, the mouth of it ringed with orange plastic. Sylvia watched the girl lift the gun, pushing it through the hole in her face, but there was nothing connected to her mouth that could swallow it. The gun disappeared into the dark of her skull.

When it was day, Sylvia walked to her aunt's bedroom and stood over her curled body. Reaching down, Sylvia scraped the sheets back and woke her aunt with a slap to her spit-damp cheek. Aunt Huilin jerked, opening her eyes and asking what time it was. Sylvia ignored her and asked, *What did you do with Baiyang's gun?* Aunt Huilin closed her eyes. Her eyelashes forked into the dark, parting it. She tucked her lips between her teeth and pretended to be asleep. When she didn't move again, Sylvia left her aunt in bed and walked to the closet with the chair braced outside it. Her aunt always said the chair was meant to stop thieves, but Sylvia hipped it aside and opened the double doors. There was a photo of Sylvia's mother taped to the inside of one of the doors, a private portrait that was never permitted to face daylight, and Sylvia had spent years coming in to look at it. In the photo, Sylvia's mother was standing in the wetlands with reeds up to her knees, and behind her was a row of blown-open watermelons, the innards slopped at her feet. *The best aim of the whole class,* Aunt Huilin would say.

When Sylvia opened the doors, she saw that the light in the closet was on, syruped and slow to reach her. She waded forward, and behind her, Aunt Huilin was rising from bed, telling her to shut the closet. The photo of Sylvia's mother had come loose with the force of opening, and now it was on the carpet, face side up. The photograph had been pleated so many times, it looked like Sylvia's mother was striped by light, bleached by creases. Sylvia, too, knew what it meant to fold a feeling into its smallest form, to grasp at something that was already gone.

When Sylvia turned back to the closet, she saw a row of black garbage bags, full of holes and on the brink of birthing. Behind the stacked garbage bags, looming like a body, was the mattress with Sylvia's stain still stamped into the right side. The mattress was yellow and sagged in the middle from years of bearing all their bodies. Sylvia wondered how she'd ever been able to imagine it a boat, something that could float.

Aunt Huilin was beside her now, trying to knee the doors closed, though Sylvia had already seen everything: the garbage bags of Baiyang's clothes, everything Aunt Huilin claimed to have thrown away, the shelf along the back wall where his shoes stood on top of hers. Sylvia remembered her saying she'd throw those shoes to the neighbor's dogs and let them shred the soles, because it was still more honorable to be a bitch than a soldier.

Sylvia saw Baiyang's gun on the shelf above the shoes: Its plastic mouth had been brighter inside the ghost-girl's hands. She reached up, sliding it off the shelf, and it was smaller than she remembered, a gun with room for only two bullets at a time. Aunt Huilin reached forward, trying to put the gun back, her hands so frantic that they snagged in her own hair.

Sylvia walked to the other side of the room, back toward the doorway. This time, when Aunt Huilin grabbed for the gun in her fist, Sylvia let go. She let her aunt take it back. Sylvia remembered what Aunt Huilin once told her: *One day I'll pay my debt with a life, and I pray it will be my own and not yours, not Baiyang's.* Aunt Huilin's hair wired the air, frying in the light. She swatted it out of her face and looked down at her hands, confirming they were still there, gritted around the gun.

Sylvia kneeled in the doorway and thought about debt, about what she was willing to pay, whether it was too late. Her aunt gripped the gun's plastic handle, hissing as if it burned to hold. Aunt Huilin guided the gun like the girl she'd been, and Sylvia saw the practiced way she was raising it now, her hands so still that the air around her seemed to be moving, splitting open and stitching together with a sea's rhythm. Her aunt squinted and shifted, knees bending in prayer, the gun opening its orange lips. Sylvia already knew what part of her body Aunt Huilin was aiming for. Even before she saw the bullet, she opened her mouth to swallow it.

The La-La Store

She pronounces *dollar* like La-La, so I say it the same. She says: *Can I get change for this La-La? How many La-Las does it cost to fly home once in a while to see me before I have a stroke and die with a mouthful of flies and you will finally be forced to come home for my funeral? I better not be dead when I see you next.*

When I was child, my mother walked to the La-La store every Sunday, taking us along only on birthdays, Christmas Eve, and New Year's. We were permitted to pick one thing—my mother held her forefinger so close to my face I had to cross my eyes—to take home as our own. My brothers were allowed two things each, because they would inevitably break one thing on the walk back, so by the time we got home everything was fair.

The La-La store was so bright inside that the sky outside looked dull and thick as a scab. The fluorescent lights silvered the floors almost translucent, and I slid my heels through the aisles like I was skating on an iced river. There were so many aisles in the La-La store that we lost one another in seconds, my three brothers dispersing, my mother standing by the counter to talk to the girl who opened and closed the cash register and counted the La-Las every few minutes. I watched the beef-pink tip of the girl's tongue when she licked her thumb. There was a piercing in the center of it, a pearl stud the size of a teardrop, and when I asked my mother if I could have one too, the girl laughed and said, *Not for sale.* When my mother left to scour the aisles for canned soup and powdered milk, I propped my chin on the counter and asked the girl if she'd ever swallowed the pearl or if she just carried it loose in her mouth like a moon. *No,* the girl said, flipping her tongue with her fingers so I could see its underside. *It's sewn into me so I can speak.*

Past the counter, there were aisles of sunglasses with lenses in the shapes of stars, hearts, La-La signs. There were composition books for school and furry-faced notebooks that clicked shut with magnets and put a plastic lock on your language. There were handheld radios that could never land on a channel without static. There were coloring books with four-packs of crayons taped to the covers. There were tubs of markers, their colors found nowhere else but inside this store, a blue so deep it was the color of closing your eyes, a yellow so bright it made you cry. There were mini-basketball hoops you could hang on the back of a door. Packs of glowsticks my brothers broke inside their packages without paying, lighting the aisle every color of a stoplight. There were bags of hard caramels with white stripes that stuck to your molars and didn't dissolve for months, and by then you had a cavity, a hole fat enough to fit your fingertip. There were plug-in bedazzlers that showed a girl on the packaging, a girl rhinestoning a unicorn onto the pair of jeans she's wearing. There were battery-powered handheld fans that my brothers dared me to hold close to my face while sticking out my tongue, the plastic blades battering it until the tip purpled and the battery died and my mother banned us from buying any more fans.

I always walked to the back wall of the store, where there was a revolving stand of plastic keychains with names bejeweled in cursive. I knew my name didn't live on any of them, so I looked for other names to adopt: Today I chose a keychain with its name splayed out on a beach at sunset. Behind me, I could hear my brothers calling to one another from different aisles, their voices high enough to harmonize with the fluorescent light. While we waited to check out, my youngest brother and I stood at the revolving stand by the door, its smudged plastic shelves carrying Abridged Classics with spines so skinny you couldn't read their titles. We read the first page and the last page and then switched: Today I had *Journey to the Center of the Earth* and my brother had *A Tale of Two Cities*. Then I had *Robinson Crusoe* and he had *The Legend of Sleepy Hollow*. I asked my brother for the plot of his and he said it was about a man with a pumpkin for a head. He asked for mine and I said there was an island, but I hadn't read far enough to know what happened. When my mother heard, she told me to put the book back because islands were bad luck: They floated on the sea like sailboats, and if anyone made a hole too deep in the ground they would sink. That's why, she said, in the city where she grew up, they killed trees every few years, so that the roots didn't grow too deep and puncture straight through the bottom of the island. The palms burned for days, and the air was so opaque you couldn't see your own mother if you were nursing from her breast.

After my mother paid in La-Las—my oldest brother bought the abridged *Heidi* and yodeled as we exited—we walked home slow so that everyone driving on the road could see what we'd bought. I hooked my finger through the loop of my keychain and spun it around like a lasso. My two younger brothers unwrapped a Ping-Pong set and were trying to fit the balls in their mouths. They'd each bought a plastic pistol to shoot at the cars, the foam pellets nicking windshields as the drivers swerved and cursed us. The pistols would be empty by the time we got home, one of them permanently jammed, and my brothers would try to reload them with bullets of macaroni that my mother had bought at the La-La store. She'd tell us not to fire any more food or dinner would be a wound. My mother was ahead on the sidewalk, carrying her purse at her breast like a baby. She made my oldest brother carry the plastic bag of pasta and brined peas, the cans clanking and orchestrating. We watched her back, a back so broad it dammed up the whole sky, withholding the sun from us. I said my new name and tasted the sweet of its two syllables, circling it with my tongue, and when we got home, I'd loop the keychain around the shower ring where all my other keychains hung, where every name was mine. We walked home, our shadows italicized on the sidewalk, our feet slanting the street. My brother, I forget which one, asked what the center of the earth even looked like and how we would get there, and I said how do you know we aren't already there.

MYTHS

Nüwa

The freight train began running before we were born, and sometimes Meimei and I liked to stay up and sit by our bedroom window and watch it come and come. I fell asleep sometime before the train needled its way through the night, sometime between the moon and morning, but Meimei stayed awake to watch its eeled body follow the tracks like a finger tracing a scar. From our bedroom, you could see the chain-link fence like a collar of razors, keeping the train from hipping into our houses.

One night, Meimei pinched me awake. *It had eyes,* she said, and I thought she meant the moon. She crawled out of our window and coaxed me out. We knelt in the browned grass, the night opening above us like an umbrella. Then I saw the braid of blood. Thinking it was a snake, I yanked Meimei back by the shirt collar and stepped on it with my heel. It spread itself, puddling on the grass sweet as jam. Meimei pushed me away. *Blood,* she said, and it coiled into rope again, unwinding all the way to the fence like a fuse. We followed it, climbing over the fence and onto the gravel. The blood-rope threaded itself under a bush gowned in soda cans and shimmied out of sight.

Meimei walked toward the tracks. I tugged her back by the wrist, told her the train could repeat itself any minute. But she pointed at the rails, raised like molars and glowing. They were spit-slick, but there was never any rain to make them that way. Together we walked forward, our hands outstretched as if nearing a nocturnal animal, and we stood where the train had passed. The rails were greased with blood, our shoes sponging as they soaked it up.

The train's bleeding, Meimei said, and maybe it was true. I imagined the train dragging its entrails behind it, slitting its belly on the blade of the tracks. Meimei knelt again, stroked up a wing of blood on the metal, brought her thumb to her mouth and sucked. *It's wounded,* she said, and I said it deserved to bleed. It was the train that etched earthquakes, that woke our mothers and made them so tired all day that they diced their fingers instead of the daikon.

I saw its eyes, Meimei said, and I told her all trains had lights on the front of them, to warn whatever was ahead to run. But Meimei shook her head, disagreeing. *They were eyes.* But maybe, I said to Meimei on our walk home, the blood all over the tracks and in our yard was the girl's blood, that one dead girl who'd been found in duffel bags. Meimei asked me how come the blood was just coming now, and I said sometimes with a death there's a delayed reaction, like sometimes it takes a long time for the blood to come back once it's been cut loose. It doesn't want to come back, to be bricked inside a body, to be shown a shape. It wants to snake away and breed with other red things.

. . .

There was a sign hung by the city on the chain-link fence that said FINE FOR DUMPING. But we dumped anyway: box TVs that didn't turn on unless you concussed them, beer bottles battered into crystalline bits that the birds pecked up like seed, sofa cushions browning in sweat, Hot Cheetos bags that the wind fed full again, bras missing their clasps, a headless tae kwon do trophy, knuckle skin.

We dumped even what we loved: Mrs. Hua scattered her husband's ashes by the tracks and later we went digging for a geode of bone or a silver-capped molar, none of us having ever touched human remains, not counting the time the Baptist priest's daughter died and her funeral was open casket and our mothers forced us to kiss the chemical-candied cheek of the dead girl, unripe and fist-like. *This is why Chinese people don't do open caskets*, my mother said. *We look ugly dead. Plus it's selfish to bury whole bodies. There isn't enough space in the ground for everyone's family.* But we'd seen our mothers bury things by the tracks: unripe babies in duct-taped cookie tins, wedding rings, cans of cash they promised to dig up later to send us to school but were instead digested by earthworms and defecated into mudslides. The dump outgrew its fence, outgrew us too, and I dreamed at night of setting it on fire, a pyre swapping out the sky with smoke.

When the girl was found by the tracks, her body was in three duffel bags. I heard later that the girl's sister identified the body just by looking at the limbs alone. I started looking at my little sister's arms and legs, wondering if I'd recognize them alone. I chose a different part of her to look at every time she came home: *Good night*, I said to her left kneecap. *Hi hi*,

Meimei, Meimei, I said to each of her elbow hinges. Meimei said it was a shenjingbing thing to do, said I should look her in the face when I'm speaking to her, but I say when her face gets shucked off by a coyote someday, she'll thank me for identifying her body by its shinbones.

Meimei and I worked at the salad bar of a retirement home where my mother did the cleaning. At noon we scooped canned tangerines and bruised beets and lint-colored lettuce into Styrofoam bowls. We wrapped foam around fork handles to help facilitate fingers into fists. All the food served in that cafeteria looked pre-chewed, the kind of grit that mother birds spit into the beaks of their babies. We crushed the croutons with a mallet, grinding them into sand. Meimei liked the people, but I was afraid of their catheters, bright as glowsticks once you've broken them. Our mother said retirement was an American idea, that our grandmother on the island worked in an infant-formula factory until the day her bones got recalled and she was dissolved into a flock of white crows.

One of the girls who worked in the kitchen was named Vivian, and her job was to cut raw chicken into slices so thin you could drape them onto a piece of newspaper and read the headlines through them. Vivian dressed guy-like, her cargo pants slung low so I could see the brim of her boxers, the knobs of her hips copper-slick, her hair stunted at the back. A silver canine I wanted to suck like salt candy. Hands that shook when they weren't holding something, so she holstered them in fists with the thumbs tucked in.

After we served lunch in the dining room, where the carpet sank like bread beneath our feet, Vivian and I spent our breaks in the backseat of her 1992 navy Subaru. She claimed she could read palms, but when I gave her mine, she kissed my palms instead of reading them. She said my hands were designed to catch the rain like coins, even though it never rained. Her hands smelled of raw chicken and vinegar and mine smelled of her spit. One of her cheekbones had a birthmark perched on it. I covered the blue spot with my thumb, felt her bone tremor beneath the skin, a seismic shift that lifted the car two feet above the street and collapsed every stoplight in a two-mile radius and temporarily dislocated the train tracks, jolting them into the shape of her spine.

On one of our breaks, Vivian told me this story: Nüwa was the woman/serpent/snake/snailgod who created all humans. She molded them by hand from yellow clay, but one day she got carpal tunnel and decided to do it a faster way, by dragging a rope through the mud and flinging it up. According to Vivian, there are two kinds of people, those who are touched by Nüwa herself and those who are raised by her rope, flung like dung. Vivian didn't have to tell me which kind we were. I knew a man on my block who hanged himself in his garage one summer with his daughter's jump rope. My mother said that for a week before it happened, she'd seen him standing in front of his kitchen window, watching for the woman who had left him, a woman who one time ran to our door in the beginning of night with a broken nose swelling big as a tulip bulb. If you cut open a tulip bulb, my mother told me, there is a baby tulip inside it, whole and tender. I saw the bone of the woman's nose and there was no miniature nose beneath it, no new one to water back.

My mother sat the woman down in our kitchen and poured rice wine over her face, and when I tried to turn on the lights, my mother told me not to watch. We sat there in the dark, Meimei and I squinting from the doorway of our bedroom, while the woman kept trying to touch her nose. My mother slapped her hands away and told her to breathe through her mouth for the next month. I might have imagined it, but my mother bent forward and spat right onto the woman's nose, her spit thick as honey. *Spit on a wound and it heals into a mouth.*

I told Vivian there was another way to tell the story of the world, which was the way my mother told Meimei and me: In this version, Nüwa had a baby with another god and gave birth to a baked ham. The baked ham was cut to thumb-sized pieces and sprinkled over the earth to populate it. *So you're saying we're made of ham?* Vivian said. We were sitting reclined in the backseat of her Subaru, the seats radiant with our sweat, and she said, *I don't even eat ham.* I told her she could look up the story if she wanted to.

Believe this one, I said to Vivian: Once, Meimei and I followed a rope of blood to the tracks. The next morning, Meimei went out with our bath towels to wipe the rails clean of blood, then walked around the tracks, looking for stones the size of her head to start sanding down the rails, dulling their edges so the train wouldn't bleed when it rode them.

Vivian suggested we stay out and watch for the train together: Under certain moons, she explained, it was possible for light to undo the shape of you. There was a story about a white snake who reversed from woman into reptile when the moon was the width of a splinter. *This is a sad one,* Vivian said. I told her I didn't want to hear the ending, so Vivian made me a beginning, got between my knees and crowned me.

At home, our mother was watching her favorite TV show on the Chinese channel: a talk show where two identical brother-hosts interviewed the mothers of disappeared children. Usually they focused on domestic stories, but today's show was a special about families that sent their daughters to the States to study. The daughters went to study in places we associated with white things: blizzards, dairy, people. The daughters were fifteen, eighteen, twenty-three. Their daughters wore glasses or not, were single or not, were smart, had never worked at a salad bar, loved birds but only yellow ones, pursued landscape painting, enjoyed eating fried crickets, had dandruff, had eczema on the third and fourth knuckles of the left hand, came home every summer with duffel bags full of Fruity Pebbles and multivitamins to gift all her aunts, wore only blue, had gotten her belly button pierced in secret, had been sleeping with girls for several years, was still unfound, was found but unidentifiable.

I fell asleep during the final segment, when the host was analyzing some kind of satellite photo, but my mother kicked me awake and told me to listen. *If you don't open your eyes now*, she said, *you could disappear.* I said it was unlikely, that I knew all the rules the show hosts were saying, about strangers' cars and secondary locations, but my mother said it wasn't enough to know things. *You have to swallow what will happen*, she said. *You have to hold all possibilities hostage in your belly.*

At the end of the show, before the credits rolled, the screen flashed a recommended list of things to bring when visiting the States: Mace. Bear spray. Flashlight. Duct tape. Blade. Identity documents. Emergency contacts. Painkillers. Nonperishables. Empty suitcases for bringing gifts back home (but not a suitcase large enough to be stuffed into).

Every night, my mother told me this story: Several seas ago, the women of our tribe hanged themselves with their own hair to avoid being captured by the Qing Dynasty/Dutch/

Japanese army, and even after the bodies were cut down, their hair kept growing from the branches, vining and perming into a generation of snakes, a lineage of spines. *Don't whistle at night,* she said. *The snakes will arrive and wreathe you. They don't remember us anymore. They don't answer to their names. They will fang into anyone they find.* When I was little, I didn't believe this story: There was nothing on TV about those women, and no one could interview a tree or film its grief. But, my mother said, there were lots of shows featuring men who wreathed wild snakes around their necks, thumbing open their mouths, flirting with the fangs. *Because they don't recognize who those snakes are,* my mother said, *and they don't fear.* They can't trace the snake to its stump-root, the place where it's been severed from its woman, forced to live forever as a forgotten limb.

I hated this story, but Meimei always wanted to hear it. She opened our window at night and triple-licked her lips and whistled, even though I said there were no snakes out there. It was too cold. But she kept whistling, rhyming with the train as it came, summoning all our mothers.

I didn't realize I knew the girl found by the tracks until I saw her photo in a temple newsletter. There'd been a funeral. The photo was from years ago, so she looked exactly how I remembered her, a short-haired girl with scabbed lips and frond-like fingers that skimmed my chin. We played together once in the crawl space of her father's two-story house, back when my mother moved us into the neighboring duplex for a summer, saying she'd always wanted intact windows. The girl asked me to teach her guoyu since her mother wouldn't, so I taught her the things we said rarely. When the rain is light, we say it's feathered. We don't say there are loose ends to tie up: We say there are chicken feathers all over the floor. *We are a meat-minded people,* I said. *When you see me, ask if I've eaten.*

Eaten what? she said, and I said, *Anything. Have you eaten?* I asked her, and she said, *Yes, you.* She gnawed at the end of my braid until it was a forked fuse, touching it to her father's cigarette lighter. But we didn't know that wet hair didn't burn: It smoked up our noses but rendered no light. In the crawl space, we found a dead cat that had dissolved to the teeth. The prettiest thing was the spine, slack as a pearl necklace, which she wanted to bury in her backyard. She got the closest to the body, almost nosing the bones. I asked her if she wasn't afraid of catching some disease, but she said we can't get diseases from the dead. When her grandmother died, she didn't want to hold her sore-spangled hand, but her father forced her to. *This is the last time you will ever get to touch her,* he said, but that was a lie, since he also forced her to kiss her grandmother's cheek during the funeral. *It was hard and kinda sticky,* she said, *like a caramel apple.* I explained to her, *We don't touch the dead directly. We do portraits and look at when you were most beautiful.* She asked me if I could take her death portrait, and I said we didn't have a camera.

That's okay, she said. *Just look at me. Really hard. Remember when I looked like this.* Knuckle to knuckle in the crawl space, I looked at her a long time, at the mouth that I kissed once and only in the dark, before she turned her head away and said we shouldn't be doing this, her father was in bed somewhere above us, and he could hear through the plumbing, he recruited all the sinks to be his ears, so I turned away too and pretended I hadn't started it, hadn't asked her to see her crawl space in the first place, which was really for torna-does, even though there were no tornadoes here, only earth-

quakes, and in an earthquake we'd definitely be dead, our
spines crushed and scooped up like sugar, and when I shut my
eyes and opened them again, I said, *There, I've taken it, your
face.* She said, *Good,* and told me that when she died, we
wouldn't have to touch. I would only have to unzip my eyes
and formulate her face in this dark. *No one would ever know,*
she said. *How I roof you.* We played practice-burial, this time
without the cat bones, and she rooted herself deep, to the
hinges of her knees. I played her portrait, crouching the way
we did when we kissed, her throat lanterning between my lips,
my eyes shut to see her.

Vivian said I lacked a fate line. We were sitting on the sidewalk outside the tracks, my hands huddled inside hers. She
bladed her thumbnail down the center of my palm, halving it,
and said this was where a fate line was supposed to go. But the
one on my left hand was perforated like a sign-here line, and
the one on my right had gone missing, had stitched itself into
someone else's skin. *I don't need a fate line,* I said. Mine was
forged by her finger, tailored by her touch.

What do you believe in? she said. *Not my hands,* I said. It
was evening and someone was roasting a pig outdoors, the sky
lined with char. Vivian said she never believed in palm reading either, until one time her aunt from Miaoli predicted that
Vivian would be born again in this life.

Don't you mean born again in the next life? I said. Vivian
puppeted my hand around, walking my fingers along her legs.
No, she said, *in this one.*

It was too dark to see her face now, and the streetlights
never came on. Behind her I could see the chain-link fence
that barricaded the tracks.

It's Nüwa, Vivian said, rubbing my knuckles. *She's come back to reverse us.* I told her that the train had no eyes, just bruised lights, that it only knew how to thread itself in one direction. But Vivian looked back toward the tracks and said I didn't know how many lives it had.

I was the one without a fate line, whose future was threadless as the sky, but it was Vivian who disappeared. It was fall and raining for the first time that year, a rust-colored rain that scabbed over the streets, and when I went to work at the retirement home, Vivian wasn't there. It was a week before we heard her mother was looking for her, that her cousin was in the hills with a headlamp on. Vivian's car was parked at home, which meant she had walked somewhere, and her cousin— who told my cousin—said Vivian was probably following a road parallel to a palm line.

After work, Meimei and I drove down to Vivian's house, where the paletería next door had a pink-maned mechanical pony you could ride by feeding a dime into a slot in its mouth. Meimei and I used to pass it on the sidewalk and pet its muzzle, feed it the ripe carrots of our fingers. Vivian's house was painted tongue-pink, and her mother answered with a cleaver in her hand, said she didn't want to talk to any more reporters. But there hadn't been any reporters covering Vivian's maybe-disappearance. Behind Vivian's mother, we could see her cousin on a sofa embroidered with dandelions, emptying the batteries out of a headlamp. *She's always been a flake,* her cousin called out to us, before the door shut.

Meimei said we could make flyers and staple them to poles and trees, just like they did in movies, except I didn't have a photo of Vivian's face. I shut my eyes to see her, to fish out the

shape of her face, but all I saw was the back of my blood. Meimei and I sat on the curb outside the train tracks, our sweat
curdling our shirts, and when it was night we walked the
tracks, waiting for someone to tell us to go home, that we must
be missed somewhere. We kicked at the cans, listened to their
silver mouths crumple shut. Even though I told her not to,
Meimei bent down and picked up shards of beer-glass with
her bare fingers. I spat on her fingers to heal them. Then she
jerked back from the glass, pointing at the ground: It was the
blood again, a rope of blood as fat as our forearms, reeling
away into the dark.

We followed it, ran parallel beside the tracks, swerved
around a car bumper bent so bad it resembled a mustache. The
snake of blood assimilated into the black, left our tongues
hard-edged with the taste of iron.

It was quiet except for the houses herding their people to
sleep, except for the sour-mouthed sound of a child being
spanked with something that wasn't a hand, maybe a wire
hanger, maybe a rolling pin, a thing that Meimei saw in a
store once and thought was a massage roller. *Look*, Meimei
said, and pointed to the ground, where the blood-snake
whipped between our feet before it fled, flickering away, leaving behind something bright. I thought it was glass again,
something that glittered more when it was broken, but it was
a knife. Putty-handled, dull, like the knives we used at the
retirement home to slice the chicken breasts thin. I reached
down for the handle and felt the heat of Vivian's hand.

We heard it from half a mile away, the ground bucking, the
houses cracking their joints. It ran straight as a blade, lighting
the air, and when its head butted out of the dark ahead of us,
I saw its eyes, its tongue silver and prodding. I dragged Meimei away from the tracks, stumbled into a brush of needle-

leaves, but Meimei stood up and walked to meet it, saying,
Nüwa, Nüwa.

Meimei stepped forward and reached out her hands to
stroke the coming train, a coppered mouth, a snake sliding forward on its greased-up belly. Kneeing her in the stomach, I
folded her up and pulled her toward the bushes, the fence.
Then I stood by the tracks and waited for the snake with my
knife held upright like a hitchhiker's thumb. Waiting to hitch
myself to another body's hunger. The snake rolled forward, its
fangs the height of a house. Along its sides, scales hinged open
and shut like doors. I prayed for the moonlight to stroke the
snake in the right place, to touch it the way Vivian touched my
palm, just once but with the tenderness of pressing a beetle
into green glitter with your thumb.

When the snake shot past us, I flung the knife at the blur of
its body. I wanted it to stop and look at us, to look at this city
with all its missing, and the snake reared its head, whined
smoke. It toppled off the tracks, gravel raining backward into
the sky, the street behind us crackling like raised bread. The
whole length of the train, oil-dark and heaving, beached beside the tracks and hissing with its mirror-toothed mouth.

Meimei was behind me, pushing me forward, running to
touch it with both hands: *A god a god a god.* There was something rippling inside its belly. It derailed in front of us, its
scales molten beneath our fingers, a dark taffy I slit open with
the knife, Meimei beside me saying, *Be gentle, be gentle.* Embedded in the snake's plum-flesh were knobs made of bone, so
white I was afraid to touch them, to make a fist around such
light. I thought we must be seeing its spine, but Meimei said,
It's a door. With both hands, she grasped the nearest knob and
tugged until the bone dislocated, sliding out like a drawer.
Laid out on the bone-tray was Vivian, her arms slimed to her

sides, her hair balled up in her mouth. We dragged her out onto the tracks, slicking the gravel, the grass. Tugging her by the feet to the chain-link fence, we measured her breath by placing pebbles on her chest and seeing if they rose. They rose. We looked back at the snake. It writhed on its belly, zipping its skin snug again. When the night folded down its slats, the snake slid back onto the tracks and siphoned into the dark, sleeved in some other city.

We leaned Vivian against the fence and slapped her cheeks. She woke up and mouthed at the air, saying her own name, moonlight crusted to her face like snot. While Meimei rubbed her hands and feet, I searched for blood, for some evidence of the snake, but all I found were confetti-shreds of flesh steaming alongside the tracks. It reminded me of the time Meimei and I found six half-rotting watermelons in the dump. When Meimei kicked an eye socket into one of the melons, flies ribboned out of the hole, frenzied by their own sweet scent, colliding with our mouths and playing tag with our teeth, fastening to us and becoming our skin.

Don't touch anything you aren't willing to swallow, I said to Meimei. She stood beside me and reached down, plucking a streamer of snake-flesh off the tracks and lifting it to her lips, flies orbiting her head like a negative halo.

After we suctioned her out of the snake-train's belly, after she woke and went back to work and paid to replace the knife I'd stabbed into the snake, Vivian tried telling me the story of how she wanted to surprise me and take me out to the tracks so we could watch the train come, maybe beg it to stop and carry us wherever it was going. When she followed the blood-rope to the tracks, the train was there with its womanwide mouth, its light fanging into her. But she didn't finish the story. She barely spoke anymore. She believed everything the width of her wrist was a snake. Nearly took the arm off one of the ladies at the salad bar, who tried reaching for the arugula. Another time, I caught her in the parking lot with a cleaver, hacking a tree to pieces, believing it was a snake staked vertical. The leaves scabbed over her skin, crusting to her calves, and I bent to pluck one up. I remembered what my mother once said about encountering the dead: *At funerals, tuck a leaf into your pocket. Its life will fend off death, but when you leave, discard the leaf immediately—a ghost could be cleaved to its underside, trying to follow you.* Vivian shook out her limbs, shedding the leaves like scales, and I wondered if she was the one souring the life inside them, if she was a ghost seeking skin to live in.

Vivian wore slats on her skin, bars of shadow that pleated her cheeks, and I knew there was a new face growing beneath this one, waiting for the first to shed. I asked her if she'd met anyone else inside the snake, if she met a girl cradling cat bones who could only be seen with shut eyes, but Vivian said she only remembered a face blank as her fist.

After the lunch hour, we fell asleep twined in the backseat of her car. When I woke up, her mouth was muffled against my arm, biting it to the bone. She bandaged it later in the walk-in freezer, wrapped the wound in butcher paper, made me promise I would never be eaten, never go back to see the train when the moon was motoring it, where the light would mosaic my skin into scales.

I hear they got the train rerouted through another part of the city, that one of the petitions about unreasonable noise finally went through. Meimei said the train would eat other girls in other cities, and though we scanned headlines and skylines, there weren't any reports. But we knew it didn't mean the snake was full enough to forget us. We just knew it meant no one wanted to write the names of the swallowed, so we did it, writing every name we could think of. Vivian said there was a better way to write: by tying ropes around our waists and running in shapes, dragging the rope through soil we'd hosed with our own blood, our palms opened like envelopes. We ran in zigzags and circles, the ropes around our waists tailing through the mud, spelling out the shapes of our shadows, writing out our names big enough for the sky to pronounce whole.

Eating Pussy

Her name was Pussy, but the rumor was she didn't have one. One of the boys, who was named Dunkin because that's what his parents first saw when they got to America, a Dunkin' Donuts, said that all she had was a bush down there, a burning biblical bush like the one Moses saw, and we wanted it on fire. We all laughed about her FOB name, Pussy, though our names were things like Penny, Pity, and Purity. Mine was the worst, Pity, and there wasn't even a good excuse for it, because my parents learned English at school in Taipei, their classroom docked in the shadow of an American military base, where GIs parted the skirts of schoolgirls, revealing a red theater of thighs. My brother's name was Pride, but my friends said he didn't have any. He used to dive for recyclables in the Taste of Jiangnan dumpster and spent all his quarters on Yu-Gi-Oh! cards, battling all the boys at lunch for a holographic one, though I said, *If you want something shiny, I'll buy you a roll of tinfoil and skirt you in it, I'll punch you in the face and flick on all the light switches inside you.*

Pussy had eyes far apart like a frog, reminding me of those stories my mother told me about how Taipei used to be a swamp, and she and her twelve sisters, six full and six half, would wade around in the mud looking for frogs to eat. They tore down hot metal fences and grilled the frogs on them, lapping up the meat, scrapping over the eyes. Prey eyes, that's what they're called, when your eyes are on the side of your face and not screwed into the front. In school, we learned that's because prey animals have to see their surroundings to know when to flee, but predators only have to look forward, spotlighting what they want to eat. We looked at Pussy with all of our light. I imagined eating her eyes one at a time, first her left and then her right, the pupils like candied stones, swallow and you'll sink. Even after my mother left Taipei and her house that sank at a slant, even after she married Baba, she walked around like the ground would filter the meat off her bones, spit her ribs to the surface. She walked high-kneed and prancing, and my baba said, *That's your abu for you, living like the land's still mud.* She didn't trust concrete or asphalt, claimed that this whole city was built on a sand-filled bay, that soon the sea would avenge itself, flooding out even the sun.

Pussy started eighth grade with us, but the rumor was she had been held back for three grades and that was why she was so much taller than all of us, her denim skirts bleached white where her hips pressed against them. She carried those hipbones like holstered pistols. Once or twice I brushed by her in the bathroom, just to feel her bones like a pestle, grinding me into pepper. Pussy was so big, she was the only one allowed to play four square with the boys during recess, while we were cornered into doing shit like rhymes and jump rope, which was only fun when one of us knotted the rope around our neck and got sent to the suicide-prevention-and-anti-drug-use counselor, a woman with breasts like stone fruits, firm and blond-furred. I watched from the shade, staring at Pussy as she rolled up her sleeves and secured them to her forearms with rubber bands, lifting her arms like they were oars. Sometimes she hit the ball so hard it burst on the asphalt, bleeding rubber pulp and shimmering ribbons of silver air. When she missed a serve, she ran headfirst into the boy who'd served it to her, ramming like a hammerhead shark, which, despite being a predator, carried its eyes studded to the sides of its head. One time, Pussy headbutted Dunkin, who vomited blood into his palms and was sent to the school nurse, who was just a teacher wearing a white coat, and who made Dunkin swallow an entire jar of cotton balls to stanch the hole in his stomach.

Pussy walked home alone. I avoided the bus too, mostly because by the time I boarded after detention for not participating in a collaborative game during recess, which was all Pussy's fault, the only seats left on the bus were the ones in the back, and everyone knew that if you sat there, the boy next to you would hammer his hand into your crotch or make you hold his dick. I never knew what to do with one of those. One time I held it kind of like a screwdriver and twisted counterclockwise to loosen it, just like my baba taught me when we rehinged the door. I thought it might fall off if I did it hard enough, but the boy screamed and the bus driver made me get off at the next stop. That heat haunted my hand, even after I hosed off my palm, and my mother asked why I took a frozen chicken thigh to bed, gripping it cold in my fist.

I walked home behind Pussy, always a block behind, and begged her in my head to turn around, just once. I rehearsed what I would do: wave, maybe, but with both hands, or ask her for her name even though I knew what it was, I pouched it in my mouth, I chewed it like a petal. Or maybe I'd fall flat like

her shadow, let her drag me home by the hair, let her chain me
to her bedpost and sleep knotted at her feet. Anything. But she
never looked back when she walked or even looked side to side,
which made me think I was right: She had prey eyes that could
see all around her, while all I could see was her, and with eyes
like that, she understood what was in front of her and behind
her and ahead of her and beneath her all at once, the past and
the future, the sky and her own asshole. I wondered if she
could see what my mother saw, that beneath this street was a
swamp pearled with meat and we were soon going to sink.
Pussy walked heavily, her shoes with rubber bands around
them to keep the soles from being skinned away completely,
and I wanted to get on my knees, pluck the bands with my
tongue.

The next day, Mrs. Ngai announced that we were going to
have a grade-wide talent show and that we were allowed to
enter in teams. The winner would get a year of free lunch,
even though we were all on free lunch anyway, but there
would also be a plastic trophy with a faux-marble base. My
name had never been carved into anything. When I said my
name was Pity, people always replied, *Pretty? That's nice.* I'd
say, *No, not Pretty,* not even when I dyed my hair ash-blond
with the box dye I shoplifted from Daiso. It didn't work on my
hair, my mother the cosmetologist said, because I had to bleach
it first. *You can't dye something dark. It's like trying to paint on
the night sky. You've got to turn it light first, then the sun will
show. Next time,* she said, *let me do it,* but I was afraid of bleach,
had smelled it under our sink, the big jug. I once saw a story on
TV about a woman who drank a whole gallon of bleach but
didn't even die, just vomited so hard her stomach flipped inside out and flew out of her mouth like a parachute.

At recess, I tapped on Pussy's back while she stood in the four-square line. Her shoulders were broad as cafeteria trays, the ones we stole for mud-sliding down the hill and into the trash creek behind school. Pussy turned around, and the wind shifted, all the heat cleaving to her back. I asked if she wanted to be my talent-show partner. *I don't have a talent,* Pussy said, before I even finished the question. Up close, I realized that her eyes moved one at a time, that she could swivel one to glare down at me and focus the other on the four-square court. There were rumors she'd had her period since third grade, and that she'd already gotten pregnant once but aborted it by sliding extra-hard onto home base during PE, knocking it out of her like a nickel. But her voice was higher than mine, high as a hawk's, and there was fuzz on her cheeks like a baby. I thought for a while, looking up at her, trying to remember if I had any talents, besides the ability to hold a pack of Yu-Gi-Oh! cards at the Taiwanese stationery store and sense with my thumbs whether there was a holographic card inside. My brother brought me along like his shine-sniffing dog.

My talent is I can eat anything, I told Pussy. Desperately, I knelt in front of her and fisted the tanbark, filling my mouth with blond splinters and swallowing. It hurt, but I tried to be like the monks my mother watched on TV, the men who could helicopter their minds, hovering above hurt, while their bodies below were cross-legged inside fires or beneath freezing waterfalls, their asses pincushioned with arm-length needles. I held my breath while she watched me, praying not to vomit blood like Dunkin, and when I was finished, on my knees and dog-panting, Pussy clapped her hands. *Nice,* she said, *that's so fucking cool.* But she said she didn't understand how that was a two-person performance. I could stand onstage with jars of needles, screws, and nail clippings and eat handfuls of each for the audience below me, then swallow the spotlight too. I said I didn't know, I just wanted her to be my witness, to see what I was willing to stomach for her, the tanbark threading through my intestines.

Pussy smiled at me, her hair flailing in the air, and then she said, *I know, I know. You can eat me.* I stared up at her and said I didn't know if I could do that. *Didn't you say,* she said, *you can eat anything?* She said if I was truly talented, I'd be able to regurgitate what I'd swallowed whole and unharmed. *Do it,* she said, so I punched myself in the belly, gagging up the tanbark, my tongue scraped clean of taste. I hunched over, this time unable to stand again, and she said, *See, I knew you could do it. Meet me at the trash creek after school. We can rehearse before Friday.*

After school, I climbed over the chain-link fence and waded through the ankle-deep mud all the way to the bed of the trash creek, where one time we found the body of a dead coyote, inside of which was the body of a dead rabbit, inside of which were the bodies of an entire litter of living baby rabbits, which we set loose behind the dumpster. We visited that litter every night, until one day they disappeared and there were bloodstains, which we pretended were our shadows.

Pussy stood inside the trash creek, plucking up candy wrappers on the surface, reflective as mirrors, and licking the stickiness off them. I told her she would get sick from doing that, that her babies would be born with extra limbs or double hearts, but she waded toward me, sloshing through the mud, and called me a pussy. She laughed at that, pointing at herself, and I laughed too. Then her face slackened into seriousness, and she said it was time. *All you have to do,* she said, *is eat me. Then you can throw me up somewhere backstage, after.* I said okay, afraid to tell her I'd never done this before, that one time I accidentally swallowed the bone of a chicken drumstick while laughing too hard at dinner, and when it passed through my bowels the pain was like birthing, but that was the largest prey I'd ever consumed. Pussy smiled at me, her front teeth missing, and behind them was another row of teeth. I flinched, and she smiled wider, saying that if I didn't want to do it that's okay, she would just find another partner or do a solo performance, like squeezing four-square balls between her knees and breaking out the air inside them.

I told her to kneel in front of me. Behind her, in the trash creek, a raccoon ran across the clogged surface of the water, a glass bottle in its jaws, god of want. I looked down at her, the first time she had been beneath me, and I wondered if she ever prayed, and to what. There was a white birthmark on her scalp where her hair parted, a place where light perched, and I wanted to touch it, to thumb the tender coin of her skin. But instead I pressed my lips to it, opening my mouth as wide as I could, crowning open around her skull, swallowing until my lips touched mud and she was gone, disappeared into the depths of me, her head pressing against my pelvis, nudging me open, letting light inside. I fell onto my back in the mud, laced to the bank, and pushed her out wailing, face blank as a bullet, wound-wet and waiting to be named.

Nine-Headed Birds

My jiujiu always said I would be stolen by a nine-headed bird. The kind of bird that spurred the sky into night, looking for girls to kidnap from their beds. Technically, all nine-headed birds are born with ten heads, but one of the heads is severed, its neck hailing blood onto houses below, lashing the morning red. That's what rust is: blood born from the tenth neck. Jiujiu always said we were cursed by these birds, that they followed him all the way from Hubei. When I asked why, he told me it was because he'd abandoned his wife there. Because of this, his wife grew nine heads and a pair of wings—delicately laced as lingerie—and flew after him. *She's jealous of me*, he said. *She will eat anyone who comes near me.* Then he chased me around the kitchen with his arms planked out, his mouth screwed up into a beak, his tongue tattered from all his years of gnawing it at night. His bald head braised in sweat. He chased me and made the sound of a nine-headed bird: like a car gunning toward a cliff over the sea. I could see his ribs through the fabric of his wifebeater, his chest rattling, his skin pimpled like something plucked. Hornets were buried inside his bones, and if you shook him at night, he woke up in the morning with a mouth full of wings. According to his stories, nine-headed birds were called ghost cars because of their mating call, like anything that accelerates away. They make the sound of being left.

My cousin said Jiujiu was a liar: The woman he abandoned was not a nine-headed bird, and nine-headed birds did not exist. But I didn't believe my cousin, mainly because I'd once seen him stick his penis inside a bottle rocket and try to launch it to the moon with the force of his piss, and anyone that stupid must be a bird himself, the kind that pancakes itself on anything glass. I did not believe any of my cousins, who coordinated themselves like heads of the same bird, all of them wearing the same fist-tight scarf in the winter, giving birth in the same season, and dying within days of one another, crashing their cars consecutively or swigging pesticide from the same expired jug we kept in the basement along with boxes of broken lightbulbs and DVD box sets of pirated Jackie Chan movies that were so shaky I thought all Chinese movies took place during earthquakes.

Even my cousins' memories seemed implausibly similar, all of them claiming to have witnessed our jiujiu drive his truck into a lake and resurrect himself, though half of them, including me, had not even been born then. That day in Hubei, the sky was purple and puckered like a scar. Back then, Jiujiu worked at a factory that manufactured infant formula in silver vats. The secret was that the formula contained powdered bone, a certified source of calcium, and there were rumors that the bones were human, hand-crushed into glitter and sifted fine as flour. It was Jiujiu's job to run the vats of powder formula through an industrial sifter and pluck out any pieces of femur.

Jiujiu neither confirmed nor denied the rumors of human bone, though he did once tell us our family was descended from grave robbers, thieves who cut the limbs off corpses so that we could take their bracelets. There was a rumor that our waigong once severed a human head with a fruit knife in order to better retrieve its jade necklace, a jade so clear it was soluble in light, not a crack in it but our name. But no one was willing to inherit that memory.

The day Jiujiu drove his truck into the second-largest lake in town, the water was yellowed like an infected cornea and the workers arrived at the factory only to discover that all the vats of infant formula had been replaced with cradles, and inside each cradle was a human infant with the head of a hen. Jiujiu brought one of the hen-babies home to his wife, who we knew only as the woman legendary for being an extra in a movie we forgot the name of. In the scene, she screams from a neighboring window while the hero jumps out of a train. Later, the train is derailed by a Japanese bomb and our aunt appears again, this time as a refugee walking by foot along the train tracks gnarled and thrown like the limbs of a corpse.

Jiujiu claimed that his wife beheaded the hen-baby and plucked it and boiled it, but my cousins said it was Jiujiu who did that, and either way, in order to atone for this murder, he decided to end the family line by driving the neighbor's truck into the lake. He was sunk for three days—his urn already paved with his name—when he was seen flying off the water like one of those cormorants trained to do tricks for tourists, retrieving Coke cans and plastic rings from the pickled surface of the water and plunking them into plastic buckets.

After his resurrection—of which he had no memory, so he said—he decided to immigrate. He joked that he was on his second life, that he would never touch another bone again. During the summer, he slept outside with his wifebeater rolled up to his neck, belly and nipples exposed, a sunflower growing out of his beer can. He packed the cans with soil the color of scabs and grew things we had never seen anywhere but in cartoons and illustrations, flowers so vivid we thought they'd be screen-smooth when we touched them, pixelated up close. The air scrubbed his bare belly with its salt, and even in his sleep he could slap a mosquito dead before it could syringe through his skin.

Jiujiu once took me to pirate a movie, sneaking the camcorder into the theater by taping it to the inside of his armpit and wearing a parka. The movie was about the Rugrats, and the plot had something to do with going on vacation and getting lost. Jiujiu laughed a lot during the movie and the camcorder bounced in his lap, buoyed into the air by the force of his breath. In the end, the footage was unsellable and the Rugrats were never found. My mother said he was a bad influence, taking a child like me to do something illegal like that, but my jiujiu said, *It's not like you raised her anyway, always at work at the restaurant, always with your boyfriend on weekends, that man so skinny he's a chopstick, what else does he do but skewer you*, and my mother punched Jiujiu in the beak-nose. I never knew bone could make a sound, but his bone sang. It whistled when it broke, whistled a note so unclouded I swore it was the beginning of a song, the lyrics written somewhere on the inside of my skin. Blood hung halfway out of his nose like a rain-swollen earthworm, living there for a week.

Men are like catheters, my mother said: They drain you, but someday you'll need to rely on one. But I never saw Jiujiu do any kind of work. He saved his money in an envelope taped to the bottom of his mattress, and every week he took out the envelope and counted what was inside it and taped it back again. There were different stories about how he got the money: One cousin said it was from selling his kidney, and another cousin said no, it couldn't be, his kidneys turned into fists and punched out of his body and his liver grew legs and ran away ever since he started drinking so much, and another cousin said it was money he won in bets, because he was the kind of man who bet on everything, dogs and horses and pigeons and when it would rain and when the widowed neighbor's kidney stone would finally pass, born the color of an uncut diamond, her moans keeping us awake at night, her moan like a brick through our windows, and my other cousin said no, he didn't have enough luck to earn much, he littered his luck everywhere and we picked it up after him, and another cousin said it was inherited money from the time he turned in his landlord and burned down the house and was rewarded for being a class ally, and another cousin said why would he be rewarded with money, wouldn't that just make him as bad as the landlord, and one cousin said it was stolen from his wife, the one he abandoned, and another said that the wife had actually abandoned him first and that's why he drove into the lake and didn't die, and then one cousin said is it true she's a bird now, and another cousin said no, but most of the other cousins said maybe, because we are a family of people who are followed.

My mother's boyfriend, the one shaped like a chopstick, became her stalker and even once hid in my closet for three days, until Jiujiu caught him peeing into a potted orchid in the living room and chased him out while wielding a combination lock.

My cousin was followed by a fish-shaped cloud that for years rained only on him, and we found out it was because in a past life he had been a country that caused a drought in another country and this was the only way to atone for it, by being perpetually soggy. Years ago, a crow followed my cousin with a wedding ring in its beak, and we figured either the crow wanted to marry her or this was some punishment for having stolen dead people's rings a country ago, and either way we probably deserved it.

Jiujiu watered the sunflower in his beer can and kept it by the windowsill in the room I shared with three of my cousins, because, he claimed, the light was better where I was. Light followed me the way nine-headed birds followed him. Light like a key turning inside the soft of my eye. Light like a lock swinging into the side of my skull. With his back turned to me, he rotated the sunflower twice clockwise and asked if I ever wanted to get married. *No,* I said, *but if I had to, it would be to a woman, never to a man,* and he said this was a good idea, as long as the woman I married was not made of metal. His wife had worked in Wuhan as a traffic director for years before she met him, and she'd been hit by so many cars that all her joints were puzzled together with alloys and it was impossible for her to immigrate because so much of her was metallic. Airport security would never allow her to pass. My cousins said this was an excuse for not bringing her, but I believed him.

I believed he'd given birth to himself, because that was the way he did things, like a forgotten god: The sunflower grew overnight from a mix of soil and beer-spit, and somewhere there was a lake he spent three days at the bottom of, learning to remix water into air, learning to live unlit.

At the bottom of the lake, he said to me, *I met a nine-headed bird. Each of the nine heads was wearing a crown like the Burger*

King kind. Each of them spoke to me and said, Listen, to live you have to find our tenth head. I asked Jiujiu if he ever found it, and he placed his umbrella-broad palm on my head and pretended to unscrew it off my neck. *Found it,* he said, and laughed a corkscrew laugh, undoing his throat as it rose.

When Jiujiu had a stroke the day before his forty-seventh birthday, my cousins dragged him feetfirst from the kitchen to the hallway, which was perpetually clogged with his mattress. His face turned the color of a nickel and dropped onto the carpet and was temporarily lost. None of them admitted to it later, but when he died that night, one of my cousins flipped him off the mattress to un-tape the money underneath. Each of them suspected the other, arguing about who had been alone in the room, and the whole time they argued, Jiujiu's body was facedown on the carpet. Later, when I flipped him back over again, his face was flat and elongated like a penny rolled through one of those novelty keepsake machines, the kind of machine you find at amusement parks.

Only Jiujiu ever wanted to take me to amusement parks. *If you want amusement,* my cousins said, *just go to sleep and dream for free.* But Jiujiu lent me pennies to crank through the machine one at a time, and I loved how skin-thin it was in the end, how the penny resembled none of the presidents. I loved how easy its history was rewritten, forged into fiction, Mickey Mouse's face numbed into its side. How easy it was to convert currency into memory. Jiujiu kept his will taped to the wall, the one that said to send the money under the mattress back to his wife in Hubei, but we never saw the money again, and we watched for which cousin would be followed next, this time by the ghost of our jiujiu.

But nothing followed us, not even the neighborhood strays with bald bellies, not even wind-lifted litter. Not even our

shadows kept up behind us, which meant Jiujiu had not become a ghost or a bird or anything, and I was the one who kept
looking at the sky for something with nine heads and a tenth
one severed, who kept mistaking cars U-turning on our street
for the sound of the bird, the motorized monotone of its grief.

The thing about nine-headed birds, Jiujiu always said, is
that they bleed. They fight each other featherless. After they
kill their prey, they retrieve each other's eyes and try to steal
the meat from each other's beaks, but it doesn't matter anyway,
because everything they swallow ends up in the same belly. It
doesn't matter who eats or who starves, because they share a
stomach, and it's only because they forget this that they fight.
The wife in Hubei wrote us a letter eventually, telling us she
had long ago remarried and forgotten our jiujiu anyway, that
there was no need to send anything, but out of guilt—we still
didn't know whose—we sold our matching agate bangles and
gold-peanut pendants and sent her the cash in a double-padded
envelope. I slipped in a flattened penny impressed with the
face of Donald Duck, along with a note asking if the lake was
still there, the one he drove into, and if it was possible that it
was a trick lake, that the water was just a tongue-thick layer
and beneath it was air, air and a city, a city where all the
dead are heirs to the living, where heads never outnumber
their bodies and hunger is hunted extinct and the air is so
fertile-wet you are watered into wings.

Dykes

Ail was the girl that other people described like the weather: alternately sunny, stormy, expected to wreck something. Her hair was dyed the color of a picked-up penny. She had slit pupils like a cat's, which she claimed were natural, though I once saw her take out contact lenses in the sink, rinsing them twice before her eyes licked them in again. She wore her hair in a shower cap when we were working, which made her head resemble the fish eggs we smeared onto the tops of our deluxe California rolls. Once, she lived in the restaurant for two weeks and showered over the bathroom drain, pouring buckets of soap-water over her head.

Ail's name, unlike her eyes, was real. Her mother misspelled *Ali* on her birth certificate. *She couldn't even get three letters in order*, Ail said. *She died of a brain hemorrhage.* Ail made those two sentences sound causal, like the act of naming had been fatal, her name synonymous with a grave. When we first met, she introduced herself as *three-letter synonym for sickness, guess.*

Ail and I worked at a sushi restaurant in New China Plaza, where we injected red dyes into the raw fish to make the flesh look fresher, more edible. Our boss confused the words *edible* and *flammable*, and Ail joked about spraying the fish with propane instead. Our boss was a man from Hong Kong who only drank water after he'd boiled it twice because all water in the desert—so he claimed—was actually purified piss from sewage pipes. The only time it rained, water ripped open the seams of the sky and he lined the sidewalk with buckets, telling us to start selling rain for twice the price of bottled water.

Once when I was cleaning the bathroom with Ail, I asked her why the fish had to be redder, and she told me that's what this city is all about: plagiarism. Our salt was plagiarized from the sea. Our bodies were plagiarized from TV. I told her no one would believe the fish was any good anyway, since we were so far from any body of water. She laughed and pointed down at the toilet and said the sea was right here. The sea was whatever she named.

When I first got the job standing behind the glass window of the sushi counter, where I said *O-hi-O* to every tourist who walked in, Ail taught me how to crimp the rice and suture the seaweed skin. *Each roll should be about the width of a dick*, she said. She circled her fingers to show me. To make me laugh, she pretended to jack off the sushi every time a customer had his head down, handling his chopsticks as if they were on fire. I watched her hands, slick with rice vinegar and Windex, arranging the rice like lace around slivers of dye-injected fish. Sometimes I injected too much red dye and the fish-flesh turned veiny and flexed like a forearm.

When this happened, Ail told me to watch for the boss and then pinched up the ruined fish, folded it into her mouth, and swallowed without chewing. She said she was practicing for when she was old and had no teeth, just like her grandmother, the one who still lived next to the Taoyuan Airport and named each airplane as it spent the sky. *You have to give them names,* she'd told Ail over the phone, *or else they won't land.* Ail's grandmother thought the wings of airplanes were actually giant ears that listened to men on the runway, landing when they were called down. During our dinner shift, Ail went outside to stand by the dumpsters and roll-call everything in the sky, the pigeons, the fallen-asleep planes.

What our boss really wanted was to open a Sushi Boat. Not the kind of restaurant where the sushi revolved past you on a conveyor belt but an actual boat for customers to board. The Sushi Boat would be a vessel large enough to seat one thousand people, and it would float inside a reservoir where fish lived, freshwater and saltwater breeds coexisting, which was very unscientific, and the customers could rent fishing poles on the boat and catch their own live fish and we would slaughter and butcher them on an elevated stage. We told our boss this was unrealistic for multiple reasons, the first being that he owned no reservoir, and the second being that he had no boat. Our boss said he was working on both. He'd begun to build a boat in the dumpster-lined lot behind the restaurant, but the boat was the size of one man, and it was assembled from various duct-taped pieces of garbage: cardboard from a TV box, Styrofoam cases that arrived with iced fish, a two-by-four sawed into eight mismatched pieces, and a hull hammered out of a retired wok. It looked more like the rib cage of some strange suburban trash beast than a thing that could float, but we named it anyway, christening the ship by breaking an empty bottle of rice wine against its side. There was a family of raccoons living inside the dented hull, wedged between the cardboard bottom of the boat and the greasy tarp our boss used to cover it. The raccoon mother abandoned her children that spring, and there were four raccoon babies in total, curdled inside the boat with their oil-bright fur and their claws soft as cheese.

During our lunch break, Ail tossed them garbage instead of flinging it into the dumpster, and they ate fists of napkins and bendy straws slicked with lipstick and avocado bits and edamame skins until they grew up, faster than we thought possible, and learned to climb into the dumpster by themselves. After that, we saw them only at the end of our night shifts, and even then we only saw their eyes, moving too fast to be stars and crowding us out of the dark, those eyes constellating our lives, sequinning the night like flies. Ail and I watched the raccoons pass trash to one another and feast for hours, their hunger almost a color, until we saw one of the babies—who was no longer a baby but bigger than its mother—begin eating the boat, gnawing down the sail made of someone's apron. The raccoons swarmed into the boat, darning the sides with their teeth, and when the sun began to liquefy the pavement, it looked like they were saddling the sea.

When our last shift began, the restaurant was full and the customers were drunk enough not to care that Ail was molesting the sushi. Our boss told us not to refill anyone's water, because of the drought policy, and Ail joked about converting the bathroom sinks into horse troughs for the customers to drink from. I couldn't find my name tag that night, so I wrote my abbreviated name on the back of our boss's business card and taped it to my chest: LEE. *As in Bruce,* I told Ail when we first met. She'd been spraying Windex on the sushi mats even though the chemicals were toxic, and when I told her this, she said,

What do you care, Bruce? You're already dead. Ail and I spent
our first day discussing Bruce Lee assassination plots: Ail said
the FBI had drugged him on set. I said Bruce had flown back
to Hong Kong without telling anyone and that his plane was
still in orbit, giving up gravity.

Ail told me that in the town where her grandmother lived,
there were old Japanese houses with ghosts inside them. I
asked her what the ghosts looked like, and she skated her
thumbnail across my neck. *They're headless ghosts,* she said.
She pretended to twist off her head and cleave it open like a
melon. The customers clapped, thinking she was doing a
dance. Our boss overheard the applause and said maybe we
should do live performances too, just like at every bar downtown. *The people want to see everything,* he said, looking at
Ail's breasts. I imagined she had nipples as broad as my palms.
I'd told her this once, and she said I could look if I wanted, but
I knew all wants were weapons that could be turned on you
anytime. I thought of the story about the woman who turned
to salt when she looked back at a city. The moral was either
you shouldn't look back or you shouldn't be a woman. I couldn't
remember if the woman had been naked or not, but I knew if
I looked at Ail too long, her body would slump into a mound
of MSG.

When we'd asked the boss why he opened a sushi restaurant in the middle of a desert, he said, *The people want sushi.
The people don't want MSG.* After that, Ail bought a three-
pound bag of MSG from the Ranch 99 across the street and
dazzled his tea with pinches of it. We pretended we were poi-
soning him with powdered snake venom, that he would die a
little every day until he was completely ours. Ail said we would
butcher his body with our sushi knives, store different pieces
of him in different sacks of rice, steal all his money and his

BMW, and drive out of the desert like women in love. I'd never heard her use the word *love*.

That night, when I missed my bus and decided to follow her home, Ail and I practiced our stripping. She even let me touch her unbraided hair, which had grown all the way to her wrists. She whipped off her protective shower cap and I saw for the first time how pale her scalp was, how much it resembled the seam of fat in the slabs of salmon we sliced to the exact thickness of our lips. Our boss told us we should come tomorrow wearing shorter skirts. *Sex and food are symmetrical appetites,* he said. *The people want to be fed.* If that were true, Ail said, men would only want to put it in your mouth. In the dark of her one-room apartment, we tried taking off our clothes with our mouths. The moon broke in through the window. It was the only man in the room. Ail told me we would look sexy, but in the dark I didn't feel like a body, just a hole eating itself empty. I couldn't tell where my mouth was until Ail opened it with her fingers and tacked my lips back. She said my teeth were a horse's. I told her a horse didn't live in the desert unless there was a man riding it, letting it drink from his palms. Ail cupped her hands in the dark, slurring her wrists. I knelt and lowered my head into her hands. Our bodies moved like they were jointed together, my legs sewn to her torso, my tongue arming her mouth.

Prayers don't get heard unless you're someplace silent, Ail said to me after. *Like in a meat freezer,* I said. *Like underwater,* she said. She pried open my mouth with her fingers again and lowered her head and spoke down my throat and into my belly: a prayer I couldn't hear. Underwater, she said, sound travels so much faster, survives longer. You wouldn't think that, but it's true. If the gods wanted to hear us better, they wouldn't live in the sky but in the water. *I guess the fish get heard first,* she said.

I nodded, though I didn't believe what she said about sound. I shut my mouth too fast and my teeth scraped the skin off her lower lip. It swelled in the dark, shone like a skinned fish.

When I got home later that night, my father was asleep on the sofa. He woke up when I shut the door and made me boil the sashimi I'd brought back from the restaurant. *Our people don't eat raw things,* he said. A slab of dyed salmon dangled from his mouth like a tongue, dissolving into soap-foam. My father was a dealer at the casinos, and once, while manning a poker table, he was told by one of the players that Asians had natural poker faces. *You're so expressionless,* she'd said, *you could win without trying.* My father had said nothing, but later that day I caught him standing in front of the bathroom mirror, prying at his cheeks and lips and chin, pinning them into expressions that were all variations of the same pain.

When Ail and I talked about our fathers, we realized we could be describing the same man. We even began to borrow details from each other's descriptions: *My father is so nearsighted he can't see his own shit when he flushes,* she said. *That's my father,* I said. *Your father tried to give himself corrective eye surgery with a flashlight and fried the white of his left eye.*

We were supposed to tell customers facts about the fish we'd dyed, how fresh it was and what sea it was native to. *In Japan,* Ail said to a table of teenagers, *strawberries grow fat as teats. They fill syringes with water and inject it into the fruits until they flex. Some of them even grow faces.* When I told Ail that sounded like a lie, she said, *Let's go to Japan tonight and I'll prove it to you.*

Downtown, we walked to the Eiffel Tower and plucked out the Leaning Tower of Pisa like a toothpick and took pictures beside the miniature globe that was gooey with light and looked more like a spitball than our planet. We watched a foun-

tain show, water spewing up the sky, and looked through the
revolving glass doors where the tourists ate chocolate-glazed
strawberries from mirrored trays, the strawberries fat as teats
and glossed dark as nipples, just like Ail said. Behind us, the
spouts frothing like rabid mouths. *Take a picture of me*, she
said, and I held up my half-shattered phone. But the water was
only spittle now, and the only thing behind her was the sky.

After the fountains shut off, we walked to New China Plaza
and bought a box of on-sale strawberries at Ranch 99. We
crouched in the parking lot, waiting for raccoons to arrive, all
eyes. Ail glazed the strawberry with her spit, licking its skin all
over before eating it. She said this was called *sabering*. I told
her she must mean *savoring*, and I wish this wasn't the last
thing I remembered clearly about that night: correcting the
language of her hunger, telling her I wanted to go home, that
strawberries were my least favorite fruit, that we hadn't gone
to Japan and never would.

Ail called me a pigamist. I told her she meant *pessimist*. She
said no, I had the head of a pig and the soul of one. I was too
busy rooting around in the mud to look up and see the airplanes that lacerated the air and could sew us anywhere. I told
her I didn't need to leave, since there was nothing moving me.
Ail rolled her eyes and said I was dramatic, lapping at another
strawberry, sticking her tongue out. I pinched it with my
thumb and forefinger, twisted it like an udder. I wanted to tear
it out and bed it on rice, serve it to a stranger. Ail was unbear-
able in her minor godhood, the way she rewired words and
sold facts she couldn't prove. She was accountable only to her
appetite.

Ail pulled back, her tongue slipping from my fingers. When
I reached for her face again, she turned away. *I can say things
the way I want to*, she said. *Stop subtitling me.* I said I was sorry,

that I'd stop talking now. *No,* she said, *I wish you'd say what you want.*

Tell me what you want: It was a line she must have learned from a movie. She said it once while kneeling in front of me in the restaurant bathroom. When I didn't answer, she gripped the zipper of my black jeans and yanked it down so hard and fast it caught on my pubic hair and tore it out by the root and she spent the rest of the night dabbing my skin with her tongue. I learned from that night: Pain was the better language. It emptied my mouth into an O, a buoy lifting me out of my body.

I started to tell Ail about being lifted from your body, about my neighbor Mrs. Tai. Every night she sat on the balcony next to mine and spooned grass jelly out of a vase. She was always eating out of things not designed to be eaten from: vases, ashtrays, backpacks full of saltine sleeves. I'd once seen her eat beef noodle soup out of a plumber's bucket. I'd once seen her squeeze condensed milk out of an Elmer's glue bottle. She plucked a cigarette from between her breasts and lit it with a match she struck against the rusted railing. She always offered me one, but I said only my father smoked. Mrs. Tai's teeth were fireflies, flitting in and out of her mouth when she spoke, yellow as yolks. Every night, she liked to tell the story of how she'd almost been kidnapped. Decades ago she'd been a showgirl: *The only Chinese girl with real hips,* she said. She wore a nightgown with a pattern of crows on it, though later I'd see they weren't crows but a cluster of stains. She said that one night, when she was working, a man standing in the dark outside the dressing room knocked her out with a crowbar. Some nights it wasn't a crowbar: It was his fist, a beer bottle, a pineapple, an electric flyswatter, a nightstick, a belt buckle, a kneecap. He taped her wrists together and her mouth shut, though

sometimes there was no tape and she screamed, and sometimes she had hands to beat at his passenger window, to claw
his face raw as steak. She said she thought he was going to
dump her somewhere beside the highway, but instead he drove
her all the way to the Pacific, all the way to the coast. *I was
passed out,* she said, *and when I woke up, the ocean.* I asked her
what happened next, but she never told me. Sometimes the
man was her father or her husband or her long-gone son. She
said she crawled along the beach, handcuffed, and saw two
seagulls pecking something on the shore: the body of a baby
seal, its skin scrolled back to expose bright fat.

Ail would have asked how Mrs. Tai made it back. Ail would
have asked if she'd fought. Ail would have believed every version of the story, or at least performed a kind of math, adding
and subtracting details until the sum of it was this: the sea.
Mrs. Tai spat black jelly off the balcony and flicked her cigarette into the neighboring balcony's Jacuzzi. I knew she remembered nothing but the man, his hands in the dark, the
way she'd smelled salt when the rod punctured the back of her
head.

Mrs. Tai called me a dyke sometimes, and I told her that
was right. Born to withhold water, want. I told Ail the story,
culling most of the details, and after I was done, she got up
from the blacktop and said there was a way to get clean, to see
the sea, follow me. *Let's go to the car wash,* she said. I told her
we didn't have a car. *So let's steal one,* she said, laughing. I followed her to a 24-hour car wash behind a gas station, walking
behind her on the sidewalk. The neon sign blinked staccato as
Morse code: OPEN CLOSED OPEN OPEN CLOSED OPEN OPEN.
Another sign, written on cardboard: WE LIVE IN A DROUGHT,
PLEASE DON'T WASH UR CAR. BE A GOOD WATER CITIZEN.
Look, I said to Ail, *we're water citizens.*

A white woman was getting out of her eggplant-colored SUV, walking over to the customer booth, where a machine offered butter-free popcorn. *Hey*, Ail said, *can we ride in your car?* The woman looked at us and opened her mouth, and Ail took this to mean yes. She said, *Hurry, get in,* running to open the passenger door and wedge herself in. The car was nudging forward on the conveyor belt, entering the dark that widened like a whale's mouth, and I followed her, shunting myself into the driver's seat while the woman behind us dropped her coins on the pavement. The inside of the car was beige and smoke-stained and smelled grass-sweet.

Ail buckled her seatbelt, and I told her she didn't need to: We could only go slow and straight through. She ignored me, and I let her buckle mine too. The soap was whiter than the hotel lights, morning inside a mouth. Water bruised the windows and the brushes lowered, making the same metallic sound that Ail made whenever she ground her molars together, muttering something at her cutting board. At work, I'd told her to get a mouth guard, that she was forming a habit and would one day wake up with a mouthful of gravel, and she told me to mind my own damn mouth.

Ail closed her eyes and the car radio was playing the weather. It predicted three hundred more years of drought. It predicted the sun would shut down, the sky would foreclose, but we would still be sitting here next year.

I watched Ail lean toward the window, the seatbelt taut as the tendons in her neck when I suckled them. The radio said something about this planet shriveling into a fist, and Ail turned her head to me, her neck bejeweled with sweat. *Insects will be the last things alive on this land,* she said. *Better grow wings.* She fluttered her hands and battered them against the inside of the windshield. *Stop that,* I said, snagging them from the air. I harbored her hands in my lap. We were now in the silent part of the wash, when the brushes moved like tongues over a pelt, when there were no subtitles between us. What I wanted Ail to say: *When the car wash is over, let's do it again, let's do it until there's no water left in the whole state and every- one becomes a casualty of our thirst.* What she said: *Get ready to run,* her hand moving toward the door. I thought at first that she was going to get out mid-wash, but instead she scrolled down her window, letting the water avenge all the rain we ever wasted. It flooded our laps, soaped its tongue in the sweat between our legs. She said I should call her a god: *I can make rain without a sky.* She proved it to me by pressing two buttons down with her tongue, lowering all the windows at once.

Ail didn't come to work the next morning. I did the work of two, slicing fish so fast and without feeling that I almost served someone a sliver of my thumb. The next day, when I decided I'd leave work early to search for her, a customer—his bald head the same color as a pearl—said there'd been a girl seen lingering outside the casinos without going in, and when the security guard asked her what she was doing, she asked for the way to the sea. They'd pointed downward at the ground, and I remembered that all the casinos built private aquifers beneath themselves, that all the water here was owned. But I didn't know whether groundwater was saltwater or fresh, if the sea rose out of the ground like sweat.

You wouldn't believe it, the man said. He was looking at my breasts, eyeing the left one and then the right as if trying to decide which was ripe. *Tell me,* I said, and he finally looked at my mouth. *She stripped,* he said. *Completely. She laid on the ground naked and the security guard had to pry her from the marble, except that her body was completely stuck. Like a magnet. They just couldn't lift her.* The man said I should tuck my hair behind my ears because my ears were dainty, like petals he wanted to put in his mouth. I walked out of the restaurant without taking his order, and then I was on the street, realizing that I'd forgotten to ask the man which casino he'd been at, where he'd seen the girl, the one like me, the one who took off my shirt one shoulder before the other, kissing my bones in an order unknown to me: the heel, the ankle, the shoulder blade, the chin, the kneecap, the ball of the shoulder, the collarbone, the shin, the shin again. Back then, I shut my eyes and tried to figure out why she was doing this, why she was touching me out of order, but now I knew: She was making a place of me. She was mapping me into a city that couldn't be found.

I didn't find her that day. Everyone was a tourist, and the windows of the hotels were too bright. I could only see my own reflection in them, my face rupturing like water. Ail once said you could know everything about a person by asking them about their first memory of water. *Real water,* she said, *from a sky or a sea, not a sink.* Mine: Once, when I was ten, my father and I moved west to California for a month. It rained when we arrived, and I was surprised that it was nothing like the automated mouth of a fountain: It was top-to-bottom, birth-to-burial, following the same gravity as our grief. My father and I lived in a house with a bald backyard, and he bought us a goat from a flea market. The goat was meant to eat all the weeds and dry brush and prevent wildfires from hemming us in, but instead it gave birth to a litter of dead fetuses, each of them smaller than my fist. They were stillborn because my father was starving the mother—he thought the goat was getting fat. The stillborn goats were nearly skinless, and I could see the wicks of their veins, blue and red and green. My father said they were dead because the blood became stone inside them. They didn't have hearts of their own yet. Our goat bleated, licking its beard. It had pushed out its babies so hard that its intestines were displaced, backed up into its belly. My father massaged the goat's stomach all night, coaxing the knot of its guts back into the correct cavity, and when the rain came in the morning, the goat stood up on its own in the kitchen and brayed my name so clearly I cried, the rain crystallizing to salt as it came down.

When I gave up searching for Ail and walked home, it rained in reverse. Water sweated up from the aquifers, up through the ground, up toward the sky. Geysers uprooted the street. The droplets, big as bullets, shot up to the highest floors of the hotels and punctured the clouds, bringing them down. Within hours, the imitation Eiffel Tower limped on one leg, after the flood-river stole the others away. Fish escaped from hotel aquariums and scattered in the water like confetti, some of them silver or skinned, others marbled like meat, all of them caricaturing the sea. I waded to the restaurant and waited for Ail, calling her number before I remembered that she rarely answered. I brought two umbrellas, even though I knew umbrellas were useless against rain that flocked up from the ground, rain that entered through your feet and clambered up your spine. I waited for three hours, submerged to the waist in water, the slaughtered fish floating by. Outside in the parking lot, a new generation of raccoons had boarded the kiddie-pool boat our boss abandoned, and now three of them were oaring down the street with their tails. The raccoons were glossed with rain, and when one of the babies slipped off the prow and into the water, I saw its mother snag a claw into the rain-river and hook the baby out, a movement so practiced I wondered if the raccoons had been prepared, if Ail had warned them in advance of the rain's happening, if she reversed gravity so that the raccoons could do exactly this: leave.

Cabs bobbed on the flood-sea like metallic buoys. Tourists drowned, and the security guards of all the casinos formed a paramilitary and used their flashlights to patrol the river in groups of ten, scanning the floodwater for casualties. Their flashlights could shine straight through water, hitting what used to be the street but was now the river bottom, silted with bodies and gambling chips. My father said it was like ladling stew: The water was thick with so many limbs, so many lampposts and dogs and show cars, that it almost made him hungry. I caulked every seam in our wall, every window frame, because I knew he couldn't swim. Our apartment building detached from the ground, giving up on itself, boating on the surface of the floodwater. We woke every day in a new part of the city, under a different piece of the sky, and our only daily joy was guessing where we were before we opened our eyes.

I thought of Ail before opening my eyes, praying she was alive, praying she was responsible for the water, because otherwise it was possible she was dead, facedown or hacked to pieces by the paramilitary so that they could carry away more bodies on their homemade boats. When the paramilitary went by with their bags of limbs, I named each one, as if that would somehow lower the odds that she was among them.

One morning I saw the raccoons go by on their boat. I counted there were maybe sixteen, including grandbabies. The raccoons looked skinnier but otherwise healthy. They were speaking to each other in raccoon language, which seemed to consist mostly of blinking and tail-whipping. One

of the raccoons I recognized as the baby that had almost
drowned, and it was squatting between its mother's legs, a
bulb of milk in its mouth. Then I saw the shadow of a second
boat, three times as big, bright with men: paramilitary carrying briefcases of blood. The man at the prow took out a gun,
some kind of pistol, and shot the raccoons one by one as they
passed. I could see the dark jelly inside their bellies. A few raccoons rocked into the water, shoved by the force of the bullet,
but mostly they just slumped over. Their tails stopped oaring
and dragged through the water. I tried to see if the baby was
still alive, but the bodies were indistinguishable, a shredded
blanket of meat. One of the bullets impaled my windowpane,
and I ran to seal the hole in the glass before the water found it.
By the time I was finished plugging the hole with caulk and
glue and my own fingers, the raccoon boat was gone, and there
wasn't even any blood in the river. The water had no nostalgia,
no desire to witness anything but its own rise, its erasure of
everything named.

I don't remember what I learned from living it and what I
learned from watching the TV reports. Every night, I pretended to watch my life from another city. The reports were all
reruns, as if replaying the news could corral it into the past,
each repetition an attempt to say, *Stay away*. What I saw one
morning before there were news cameras: the Ranch 99 floating on the water, and an auntie in pajamas stepping out of the
automatic doors, right onto the surface of the river, her bag of
bok choy strapped to her back like a flotation device. She swam
with her hands, chin cleaving the sea, paddling somewhere I
didn't know. I saw another auntie skimming across the water

in a cardboard box, the one she used to sit on to sell zongzi on our street. Waving to me, she jetted forward through the flood, white hair widening into a sail, lifting her off the water.

After I saw the raccoons slaughtered, I considered building a boat of my own and paddling with my hands to Ail's apartment. But there were no materials in the house except for my mattress and my button-down shirts and my father's collection of newspapers and the lunch meats in the refrigerator. There was a night after the reverse-rain began when my father climbed into my bed and fell asleep with his face smeared on my pillow, his body balled into a fist around my sheets. I flicked the hair from his face and stroked the back of his neck, humming a children's song I must have learned from him, about a boat that thinks the sky is an upside-down sea. Even this close, the distance between our bodies felt like the one between continents.

Next door, Mrs. Tai ate her cat. She spent three days knocking on every door on our floor, asking if we had any food to spare, but none of us answered. My father once said that the real difference between people was that some clustered together during disasters, and others played dead. My father kept cans of Spam under his bed in anticipation of sudden apocalypses, and at some point in the week we began to eat it directly out of the can, without the patty of cold rice, without using any utensils. We clawed the meat with our hands and nearly swallowed our fingers. Since the water shut off, we drank directly from the floodwater, even though it gave us diarrhea for days at a time and the carpet was stained with it, a sick mosaic. My father lit candles in the bedroom, but mostly we lived in the dark, waking in the day with bruises and cuts we accrued without bothering to check if we'd bled. It was today when we heard Mrs. Tai strangling her cat with the cord of her hair dryer. The cat cried like a newborn, and for a second we thought Mrs. Tai had given birth.

We heard her crying as she cooked the cat on a sheet of tinfoil, over a fire of magazines and toilet-paper rolls. The cat had been her late husband's, a man who'd been an officer in the Chinese navy and who always maintained his hands in fists behind his back, as if he were holding a weapon he didn't know how to put down. His pockets sagged with sweat and strawberry candies he gave out to anyone younger than him, which was everyone. When he died, we saw Mrs. Tai's cat prancing down the hallway wearing his clothing, a sock or his watch or his old Chinese navy hat. Mrs. Tai pretended the cat had stolen them, but we knew she was dressing it up. She shaved a bald ring into the back of the cat's head, symmetrical to her husband's.

It was Mrs. Tai next door who told me: There were rumors of a fishgirl who lived in the floodwater, who ate corpsemeat and raccoons, who could digest even bone. In the second month of the flood, the remaining raccoons grew gills and tails and learned to live underwater, eating the corpses that stewed in the rain. The raccoons lashed through the water, their bodies dark and hairless as eels, their pupils dilated to the size of fists. At night I saw them congregating, swimming in sync like a school of minnows, their fishhook tails breaching the water, slashing at my window.

I looked out my window, the waterline perforated with floating garbage, the sky slender as the slit in a fishbelly. Mrs. Tai spoke to me through a hole my father had punched into the plaster wall. *He must be lonely,* she said. *I thought he'd stick his dick through it.* The hole was the size of her mouth, so that when she crouched in front of it and spoke, I could only see her lips, her tongue, her teeth choreographing a story. Sometimes she looked through it, and her eye was wet as an oyster, something to be sucked out of its socket. I didn't like to see her mouth in that wall. I turned away. *Someone should fish for that girl. It's disrespectful to eat the dead,* Mrs. Tai said. There was a cigarette in her mouth, one of her last, and when she spoke, ash rained down on our carpet, seeding miniature fires. I stamped them out with my bare feet, heard the sizzle of my own meat.

That night, I fell asleep with my head against the window and watched the raccoons leap in and out of the water, arcing their bodies through the night, delicate as thrown knives. I remembered a story my father told me, about fire-fishers in Taiwan and how they lured fish with only light. On the darkest nights of the year, when the moon was rumored dead, they went out in their fishing boats and lit sulfur torches, waving them over the water. Swarms of fish flew out of the sea, spearing into the net, flocking to eat the torchlight. I thought it was a merciful way to kill something, to forgo the hook in its throat and teach a fish to love what's above, to die for light. But then he told me he cried watching the fire-fishers lift their torches over the water, all the fish disowning the dark they were born in. He prayed for the moon to roll in, dulling the light of the torches in comparison, confusing the fish so that they wouldn't know which light to leap for, and then the fishermen would come home with nothing.

Those fish sound suicidal, Ail had said when I told her about the fire-fishers, during one late shift when we were flushing dish soap down the toilet to unclog it, the water turning neon. *Light is overrated anyway. If I lived in the water, I wouldn't leave. I'd go deep, a place where it's completely dark. The kind of dark you could be bodiless.* I asked her what she would do, what she would eat, but she didn't answer me. Instead, she turned away and plunged her hands suddenly into the soap-gold toilet water, flinging it up at me. I shouted and ducked, shielded my face with my arms, told her she was disgusting. She laughed, and in the mirror to the left of us, our faces flapped beneath the glass like fish.

When I woke, my forehead was pressed against the window and the waterline was risen to just beneath the sill, a hem of water that lifted and rippled. Tonight, all the raccoons were clustered in a raft formation, floating on their backs. I thought they were trying to point at something. They flipped onto their bellies and swarmed just under the water, forming an arrowed flock, swimming out.

Behind me, the hole in the wall brightened with Mrs. Tai's mouth. She told me to go find the girl. The raccoons were gone, but the surface of the water still shuddered, seizing into muscle. I opened the window and leaned out over the floodwater, bright and viscous as the meat of an eye. Across the water, I could see the broken-off tip of an Eiffel Tower, skeletal but still lit.

I held my breath, and behind me, Mrs. Tai said that the body floats on its own. Bones are honeycombed. I shimmied out of the apartment window and unfolded onto the floodwater, splaying all my limbs, waiting to become a compass. *Point me toward her*, I said to my spine. I thought of the fish that the light preyed on and prayed that the dark was dense enough to carry me. The water cinched around me in rings, tails breaching the surface: The raccoons were swimming toward me, chins above the water. Their bodies knit into a raft beneath me, lifting my body moonward. Their many-fisted hearts beating at my back. When I was finished floating, when the water felt solid as bone, the raccoons dispersed. I sank, held my breath. The water bridged over me, binding my legs together.

I stretched out my arms, unknotting the dark current ahead of me. In the water, I blinked and opened my mouth, swallowed something alive and bright. I said Ail's name. She was right about sound traveling faster in water: Her name harpooned ahead of me, ripping the floodwater.

Blading my hands through the water, I kicked deeper, the water turning colder and denser, resisting me: Swimming felt like trying to pry meat from bone, like wedging my hands into a butchered body. I kept paddling and realized that I no longer needed to breathe, that I no longer knew which direction I was kicking toward, if gravity had reversed and I was now mining for the surface.

The water was a mosaic of fish. They moved slowly, some with antlers, some carrying lanterns inside their mouths, some with scales that were completely transparent so that I could see every organ inside them. The water glowed with Coke cans and minced Styrofoam. Light was locked out, staining the surface but unable to reach under. I starfished my limbs, suspended in the water, looking down at the mountain range of trash peaks seaming the river's bottom. From between two peaks, a girl swam toward me. A raccoon-eel leashed to her wrist, pulling her forward like a chariot.

It was Ail, her hair so long it unreeled down to the bottom of the river, tapering into a singed wick. Her skin shifted as if it were made of schools of fish, refracting in every direction. Her pupils were dilated, adapted to the dark. I looked at her neck, searching for a set of gills clean as knife slits, but her skin was the same, her feet bare and unwebbed. Though neither of us was breathing, I could smell her mouth, crusted with rust.

Ail hovered in the water, our bodies horizontal. She flicked her wrist and the raccoon jetted away, its webbed paws tucked into its body. I reached out and grasped her hair, heavy as a blade, and ran my hand down the length of it, tugging her forward until our mouths met mid-word. *Didn't I tell you sound travels better down here*, she said, and her voice arrived from every direction, orchestral, echoed by the fish feasting on suspended garbage. Her upper lip wore a worm-fat scar, and I wondered if someone had tried to fishhook her. I tongued at her scar, dabbed at the tissue healed hard as a stone. As the water wove itself into a basket around us, strands of Ail's hair severed at the root, detaching into a squad of eels. They flicked forward like knives before diving. Down into the dark, we hunted them home.

Episodes of Hoarders

(as scenes from your life)

Episode 1: How to Extreme-Clean

your grandmother unloads a box of live birds from a garage
shelf   the birds are mostly sparrows she hunted as a girl
socks full of rocks she spat at the branches   sparrows fried
on a fence   feet gilded in sugar   sold in the summer one
summer   the soldiers came   after curfew   rifles
wearing socks to muffle shots   they took the doctor the one
that knew   how to cure an ear   how to pickle a
nipple   how to get rid of a baby with a fork and the right
kind of wrists   you open the garage door and the
sparrows fly out and fuck   into falcons   your grandmother
cuffs one in her fist   you hold out your hand   your
fingers fooling themselves into feathers   she says a bird in
the hand is worth   two boys in the trees   eating hair from a
nest   hair is protein your grandmother says that's why I
eat what I shave from my pits   your grandmother unloads a
box of razors   a box of variety-pack cereals   a box of

syringes for her diabetes   a box of baby blankets she
sewed the borders   a box of live bees   marrying your
mouth to honey   the bees are from a hive in the ceiling
you mistake for a god   when the bees impersonate your
grandmother's voice   when   they wreathe your neck with
sting   when the bees breed honeycomb in every wall
until the house looks like it's made of light   your
grandmother says she has an affinity for winged things   she
used to catch dragonflies with her teeth   when you say you
don't believe her she bites her own tongue in two to show
you   what it means to commit to a story   at her house in
montebello   she unloads bottles of iodine ace
bandages   wrist guards   a pair of roller skates without
wheels   hot wheels   dog toys   you have never owned a
dog   there was an island of dogs once   when the women
hanged themselves in the mountains the dogs dove into the
sea became whales and ate missiles   swimmers
submarines   once in yilan in the summer with your aunts
you fed the stray dogs on the beach and they bayed   bricks
of sound   pelts oily with sun   you pet its teeth your aunts
whistled the dogs broke their bones to
salt   dissolved   waves rolled themselves into
pearls   in your grandmother's mouth   an apple seed she
sheathed in her cheek after reading in a magazine that apple
seeds contain arsenic   keep death somewhere within
reach   she says suicide is a gene   for example the women
of our tribe who hanged themselves before men   made
trees   for example the sparrows that went extinct   when
bullets plagiarized their songs   opened their bellies and
sacked their bones take the sparrow   she says   take it take
it   raise it   somewhere it has no name   see what skies

Episode 2: Life Organizing

after she dies   you butcher the house into rooms   one
room of furniture you're allowed to sit on if you baby-wipe
your butt first   one room of furniture where your ass is not
allowed to greet the good chairs are for your
grandmother   costco cushions   made of nonflammable
material   nonflammability is important   in this country
safety   is sold   separately   one room full of remote
controls that do nothing but turn off   a TV in another
country   turn on the rain in another   sky   turn
off the news when the news is about the girl who sold her
kidneys for a _____ when the news is about the man
who kept a _____ _____ _____

    when the news is about the _____ found alive when the
___ ___ one room full of poisonous flowers you
water   convince yourself this is a form of motherhood   to
love what you can't touch   one room full of cities you've
never been to   paris is a coffee table   with a broke
leg   new york is a clock with its hands clotted at
noon   yilan   yilan is not a city but a county   a word
you can't distinguish from country   county meaning
many cities   meaning many languages to forget in   one
room full of texts your mother sent you   post-
election   *baobei have you heard?   baobei tell me
what you died today   *did   little crab, if your pee is
yellow   water yourself   boil your water for you drink
it little crab get a husband   a man can mean   you don't
have to eat the pig to know it walks   baobei your hair
wet   don't walk round barefoot or your period will freeze and
give birth to ice cubes the rest of your life!!!!!!!!!!!! baobei   hi crab
baby   you're welcome for you   stop complaining   you*

know what americans say   what doesn't kill you   will
later 是你的就是你的   不是你的就不是你的   早去早回

you open a window in a room of phones that ring your
neck when you pick up you forget your mouth   noose all
the cords   confuse the voice on the other end for smoke this
is the room of ex-girlfriends the window forgives you for not
being the sky   forgives you for mooning every stray
dog   the window forgives you for never being able to love a
woman   more than memory   the window accuses you of
releasing the sparrows   into the wrong season   the
window accuses you of weather   the window asks why you
can't be more   than your memories   the window asks why
you don't open it more often   haven't you ever wanted to
unfamily   the window wants to know why you can't name
three things to do on a weekend that don't begin on your
knees   prayer   kumquats in your palms   ash in your
hair your first girlfriend says let's do something
obscene   you ask if wearing a tampon for the first
time   counts   it doesn't though your mother
says   tampons are like grenades   you pull one out   you
blow   you and your girlfriend drive together to another
state there are cherry trees   branches spraining their
arms   the car is your mother's   while you're gone she takes
the bus two hours   to work   she works two
sections of the library most of the books are bibles some
are novels about countrysides courtships emperors concubines
all of them you have never read   in third grade a river
flooded and your mother was enlisted to fight it   on the bus
when she doesn't know the stops she counts trees   tries to
find one with her face   in the leaves   when you come home

with the car your mother says nothing   she has
never hit you not even when your grandmother said a girl
will give   birth better if she's been opened before   not even
when you pissed on her pillow the year you turned ten and
she wouldn't let you watch Desperate Housewives at 10 pm
PST   you snuck behind the sofa and watched through the
crack at the bottom   the women wearing their
hair   blond   red   colors of the heatwave   the women
wearing their houses   the women burying their kidneys
behind the house   your mother asleep when the digging
begins   when you dream the body   alive in another state
eating cherries from the ceiling your girlfriend calls calls
asks why you don't even swear   you don't   know how to
explain your body   is how it got here   all the swear
words   you inherit   begin   *your*
mother's   your mother's   your mother's

Episode 3: Panic & Anxiety Management— Your Keys to a Healthy Home

a therapist enters the house   through its backmost
hole   *that door's as worn-out as my womb*   the therapist
catalogs the singe marks on your dinner table   vases clothed
in newspaper   stained with the guts of something   you
are   the therapist in this episode is also a pilot   he lands a
helicopter on your roof and rappels down into your
grandmother's bedroom   the carpet gravestoned with
shoeboxes   nikes from the outlet store   sandals from
payless   your feet don't fit any of them   but the point is
you have a pair for every occasion   flight   war   hurling
at muggers   the point is that they're pairs   everything
that comes in twos   comes true   birth and death   body

and ghost   man and wife   woman and knife   the
therapist says hoarding is a symptom   he draws a tree on the
living room wall   the symptoms are leaves   the root is the
tree the root   he says   pointing at the hole in the ceiling
where the helicopter hangs   is an inability to let go   an
inability to leave things   alive   an inability to
organize   you show the therapist the master closet   beef
jerky drying on clothes hangers   meat hung next to a
dress   the organization here is hunger   you say while
eating   the hatboxes in the back   have hardboiled eggs
inside   you say edibility is a matter of belief   believe
you can eat any where   any time   the time you got kicked
out of a museum for peeling an egg too close to a
painting   the time you got kicked out of a friend's car for
eating the wheel the time you went to a pig roast at your
cousin's house and ate the skewers   shat swords for a
week   the house mouths and swallows its roof   the
helicopter drops a rope and the therapist climbs up   waves
from the sky   says remember to inventory   things you
can keep: what you can't live without   like
toothpaste   what you leave: things   you can imagine
yourself without   you say you don't have to imagine
yourself without   you already live off your body   you keep
the six-pack of travel-size toothpaste   you throw the rest of
the room away   the bed with its mattress hardened to a
callus   the photos of women you've never met   you
share with them   an arrangement of teeth   a way of
eating with the tongue unhinged   a way of being
disappeared   you can't keep this   here in the living room
a washing machine still in its box   you wash your clothes in
the sink   the machine in its box is helicoptering out   it
disassembles itself   only a door   you open the doors of

every room so the dark can breathe   out of your
mouth   before your grandmother dies she takes you
shopping at ross: dress for less   which she calls ross: dress for
whores   you buy socks on sale   a nightgown   can you
believe there are clothes just for when it's dark she
says   are there clothes for when you're dead   you buy a
purse for your aunt   it has a buckle in case of thieves   or
beatings   your aunts in yilan think   abercrombie
& fitch were presidents   your aunts in yilan wear shirts
that say *good mourning*   say *yankees*   don't you think
yankee could be a chinese name? one of them asks   you say
yes   why not   hang your grandmother's shirts in the
windows   every stain bleached into day

Episode 4: *Institute of Living*

your grandmother kept her hand in a margarine tub in the
freezer   amputated   *diabetes* a word you rhymed
with *athletes*   sugar sprinting through her
veins   outpacing blood when you were nine you
believed   anything sweet would sever your tongue   you
believed hands were their own bodies   owned their own
hearts   tented inside the palm   she broke her wrist as a
girl and the bones never revised themselves straight   one
summer the sugar in her blood   convenes in her brain   this
is called a stroke a stroke   is what unzips the water around
your body at the beach in yilan you backstroke   your
back scabbed with sun   it took three months to clean her
house in montebello after   you hire a professional
cleaner   the first month   one that specializes in trauma
cleaning   post-murder scenes   crime aftermath   he
tapes off the kitchen and says the floor here   is

suspicious   it seizes like skin   it earthquakes in
hualien   the day you fly to yilan for the funeral   bringing
your grandmother's ashes in a shoebox   your aunts say she
must be buried where she's born   you hail a fake taxi   you
don't know it's fake until the man charges you thirteen times
the price of flying   home   the man smiles says first time
here   you say you forget   you have a body here   your
aunts sipping suanmeitang from a plastic bag   in
montebello your grandmother kept a drawer of plastic
bags   knotted like necks   enough to choke up   oceans   an
eggplant behind the refrigerator wedged there so long   its
skin is sound   suitcases of socks she meant to send
you   your initials stitched inside all of them   her
singer sewing machine in the basement where she made
skirts wholesale   you never wear skirts   femme is
fatal   you wear a handmade pantsuit to the
funeral   plastic   opal buttons   your cousins say you look
like a country   of men   a vase of red-dyed peanuts   you
eat alone in the dark   the nuts new as your
teeth   your grandmother said never eat alone   or your
mouth's first language   will be loneliness   when she
stopped eating you knew she was going to   become a
language   when the body no longer needs itself to live   it
leaves   it trees   it grows into alone

Episode 5: Home Is Where the Haunt Is

so the smell man comes to montebello   says what do you
want out   you want the house to smell of no one when he's
done   he brings spray cans of scent   summer sea   spring
weeds   autumn essence   all of the cans are named after
seasons   he says what time do you want your house to

smell like   you say anytime   alive the house has been
hoarding your body your habits   it nibbles the
windowsills it shuns shape   the house has been nodding its
nests   a marrow of sparrows in three of the walls   there
are squirrels   you aren't sure if they're there   to breed or
die   the smell man sniffs the floor and says fishy   he asks
if your family are butchers   no not technically   though
once there was a family who abandoned their golden
retriever   moved to another city   the dog was locked in
the house for months   its shadow turned white   it shed all
its teeth   animal control came and corralled its bones   this
has nothing to do with you   have never owned anything
gold   at the drugstore you buy gold jewelry to be buried
with   you don't let anyone seal the holes in the walls where
the bees were tweezed out   like bullets   remember your
grandmother wearing the walls   knocking on the other
side   of your skin   the screen door has a hole
sewn with dental floss   you don't remember the pigeon that
flew in once and roosted inside the TV for weeks   perched
on the cables   eating its way out of the screen   now
when you turn on the TV it sings   from a beak   on an
episode of Desperate Housewives the women have affairs
with their gardeners   the gardeners have silver shears for
penises   you dreamed this   the women birth
hedges   skies   the women tell their husbands to
fly   their houses teething on fences   their walls have
no animals inside them   their closets sorted by color   no
hair hampering the drains   no toilet that doesn't flush
unless your fist   is down its throat   you make an
inventory   of everything you own   the list is just your
name   at your grandmother's funeral   in yilan you took the
bus down a mountain   the sun swung down like a

fist   broke the bottom of the sky a mirror   at the bottom of
the mountain   a cemetery   a litany of trees   red string
tied at the base of each   to keep thieves away they made
a moat   tadpoles touring the mud   all
water   grave   red thread ringing your wrist   a gold bell
goodbyeing   your necklace of aunts   give you a fist of rice
to throw into the river   today is the deathday of a poet who
suicided   who tied his feet together and sank himself in the
river   the rice lures   fish away from the body   you numb
the rice in your hand   finger it   to peaks   you feed it to
the moat   grows   a throat of water   rain stitching itself a
body   the vending machine on the street offers
socks   you swap your skin for sweat   wear the socks on
your fists   on the beach a statue of a warrior defeating the
dutch   on the plaque his name   begins with yours   the
kids shout salt   from their nostrils   a pregnant woman uses
her belly to float   out of herself   the statue is
naked   except for his teeth   the dog by his side   with a
fish in its mouth   he aims his spear at you   it lands   a
year from now   you pray and can't remember to
who   you realize the warrior   is a woman   her
loincloth curtains   your mouth   you bring a box of your
grandmother's things   to the funeral   you say they're
from her house in montebello   your aunts ask you to burn
everything you bring   without a translation   instead you
unpack a box of curtains   bought from a flea
market   haggled to dust   they sway like hips when you
hang them in the light   the curtains all patterned with
birds   rubber duckies   peacock feathers   to trick the
windows into believing   they're still sky   country
wrapped in one of the curtains   a box the size of your
palm   gold rings wearing a hand   hers   severed because

it refused to cooperate   with pain   you donate the
walls   the windows   you keep the toilet   the last
thing that touched her   the last time you touched yourself
was before   you had hands   you bury the hand on the
beach   it winces into a fist   it scuttles after you like a
crab   it pets the warrior's dog   licked clean by wind   it
swims out   makes a palm   founds an island   you flag
your hands   in the sand   your nickname   little
crab   came from her   as a baby   you pinched everything
you didn't have a name for   walked sideways before you
knew what feet were   dogs arrive at your ankles so you
feed them   they leave by sea   you've seen their hunger
before   in other bodies   you remove the moon from a
drawer of salt   exchange its face for
yours   bury its bright   walk sideways to the
city   where loss is a belonging   where you can keep
anything you want   forgotten   the crab-hand follows you
from yilan   back to montebello   you bind its claws with
your hair   boil it in seawater   eat wires of white
meat   the crab speaks from the hole   you bite into its
opaled belly   the crab says its name   your own   it
calls   your body   home

Homophone

NiNi told me her dream was to fuck a woman named after every month of the year. She said she was already halfway there. The ones she remembered best were January (named after a blond actress, but her roots were blue), July (she had hooves like a horse and liked to be held by the hips), June (July's sister, who was allergic to fluorescent light and had honeycombed bones), and August (NiNi was disappointed to learn that August's real name was Autumn and that she changed it because it was difficult for her grandparents to say or spell, the silent *n* like a suckled knuckle). NiNi was still waiting for a May or an April. Those should be easy, she said to me, kneeling between my legs, her chin glistening, one of my pubic hairs stuck to it. An hour ago, my nipple surfed her tongue. She tried to bite open the collar of my shirt, saying she'd seen it in a movie, but all she did was break a tooth, a canine plateaued into a sugar cube. NiNi wore her brother's boxer shorts, green plaid, the waistband loose. She had to walk and shimmy at the same time, which looked to me like she was perpetually wading, her hips haloed by a lake. I tugged the boxers down to her knees, shelved her ankles on my shoulders, fucked her with one of her sixteen strap-ons, some stone, ceramic, glass. When she first showed me her strap-ons, hanging in holsters, dangling from her shower rod, they looked to me like lit-up ornaments, all the Christmas trees I grew up seeing on TV and in illustrated books. My mother always told me that Christmas was Chunjie for Americans, that they spent the day celebrating the birth of some boy, and I said that sounded Chinese to me, to love a son so much that you name a day after him.

I asked NiNi why she chose me. It was Sunday, and the Taiwanese First Presbyterian Church choir next door to her apartment was singing something in cursive, all the windows mosaicked with women's faces. Every morning after we fucked, I awoke to church bells, the sound salt-white as her eyes when she rolled them back, when I entered her again and again, when my spit sutured her fingers into silver lace, when she sucked a rusted dime into my neck. NiNi laughed when she saw me flinch at the bells, telling me what her mother told her: Girls who are easily scared by sounds have committed something bad in their past lives. That's why they startle so easily in this one. Residual guilt, inherited without a name. They await punishment, ducking from the sky like a knife. *What are you afraid of?* NiNi asked me. I said I didn't know. I told her I didn't remember my past lives, did she? NiNi said, *Yes, I remember them all: First I was the sun, but then someone shot me down. Then I was someone's son, and that's why in this life, I steal my brother's underwear. Because it belonged to me first.* I watched NiNi cut her hair in the sink, scissor it blunt at the neck, the ends brittle with dried spittle. She saw me standing behind her, renting heat from her silhouette, naked from the waist up, my appendix scar unknotting into thread, and said she chose me because my name was Mei. *It sounds like May*, she said. *What's that called again?* I said, *A homophone*, and she laughed. *Yes*, NiNi said, *that's you. Homo. Phone.* She rinsed her hair down the sink like weeds, and I licked the back of her neck, the live wiring of her veins. I felt her in the jaw, in the way my mouth opened to say stop, saw, awe. *I knew you were a month of mine*, NiNi said to me, *when I met you at the temple, not reading the words of the Heart Sutra, mouthing along to the dust, and I remember thinking, you don't know the words to anyone.*

I led NiNi to bed, lugging myself on top of her, loitering my lips on her hips. I wanted to tell her I didn't remember what I was praying for, only that I couldn't read the words to the sutra the nuns had unfolded on my lap, and I remembered looking up, looking for anything I could say, and that was when I saw her, NiNi, standing beside the bell with the bronze cranes crowding it, a bell that was never rung because, according to rumor, it was too heavy, an artifact of the tenth century, and in this temple of nuns only, no one had the upper-body strength to swing it into sound. That was when NiNi crouched and grasped the knotted rope like a wick, as if she was going to light it, and pumped her arm back and forth, battering the bell into sound, butchered music.

For a second, I'd wondered if only I could see her, if she was appearing to me like those dogs of myth, the reincarnated souls of every animal you've ever helped in a past life, the one you fed from your palm or kicked from the path of a car, and she was now coming to repay me or punish me for not remembering. In her car that night, NiNi recited the calendar of her conquests, the out-of-order months, the women she converted with her drawerful of dicks. I rolled down the window, fiddling with the seatbelt she told me was unreliable, unbuckling itself every time she turned right. The wind outside was gunning toward me, and I knew I didn't have the skin to listen anymore, didn't own a name that could outlast her mouth. I was another of her months, a chronological want, nothing like love. NiNi drove me to her shared apartment, showing me the towel-curtains hanging from the ceiling that separated her from a family of seven, six sons and a daughter who ran away. *To where?* I asked, but NiNi said she never heard. I thought about years ago when I was a runaway, when the nuns let me sleep in the back room behind the Buddha, the place where they kept a second plaster Buddha, a substitute statue, unpainted and hollow, the hole between its shoulder blades where I hid my roll of dollar bills and pretended it was an offering and not something I'd steal back later. I thought about the runaway daughter when we were lying in bed together, when NiNi was asleep, when I spent hours listening for the moment when she'd wake and say, *You can go now, the bells are ringing, can't you hear,* and I'd say, *Yes, I can hear it's morning, my mouth is still a foam of you, it's like a song I swallowed all the words to, thank you.* NiNi would shut the door after me, the door scarred with someone else's surname, and I would wonder if she'd come back to the temple and find me, or call me again, or if I'd walk past her building and climb up its walls and impersonate her window, translating all her light for her, fingering it flat, hammering out her nights. But for now, I wondered: Where did daughters go when they disappeared, and what would NiNi do after she finished fucking every month, what came after touch. She was asleep, but I turned toward her, her boxers sogged around her ankles, hemmed in sweat, her nose knighted by the moonlight. I wrote my name with my tongue between her shoulder blades, transcribed it the way it was given and not the way she wanted it, Mei, trimmed of any synonym for spring, silvering each stroke with my licked thumb, respelling my name into stay.

MOTHS

Resident Aliens

When the power goes out, we hang knives from the ceiling as substitute lights; when our beds are hungry, they bake us into bread; when the bills arrive as a flock of carnivorous birds that threaten to peck out our intestines, my mother and seven aunts and I share two bedrooms and rent out the basement—what had once been a slaughterhouse, with hooks that snagged on our shadows and no windows but our mouths—to a series of widows who respond to our Craigslist ad.

The first widow came with a collection of wigs—colored to match any weather, any cloudmood—and refused to use the toilet, saying that she once knew a woman who drowned her baby in a toilet. Instead of using the toilet, the widow pissed into quince-tea jars and shat in a series of Nordstrom Rack shoeboxes that she duct-taped, saran-wrapped, and then buried in our backyard.

The first widow sleepwalked, and one night I followed her to our bathroom, where she stood hook-spined over the toilet and wept into it, attempting to flush down her own hands, which resulted in the toilet being clogged, which resulted in my aunt calling the plumber, who extracted the widow's stuck hands with a pair of oversized pliers.

Years later, I read that a European euphemism for excrement is *nightsoil*, and for months I would repeat it to myself, *nightsoil*, a memory of the first widow walking up from the basement with a shoebox swaddled in her arms, the way she would dig a grave for it and go back to her bed with dirt-charred hands, the word *nightsoil*, *nightsoil*, as if the sky itself were made of soil and the stars were seeds I had sown.

The second widow was a florist at the corner stand by the church. She sold white carnations at funerals and taught me how to plant tulips at the right time so that they'd open on my birthday.

When the second widow married again, she sewed a dress of stems but forgot to de-thorn some of them, so by the time she reached the groom, her skin was hole-punched, worms emerging from each of the wounds, like the kind I used to pluck up from the sidewalk after it rained and rebury before the birds could eat them.

The third widow was a butcher and said she liked our basement because of the meat hooks, which reminded her of earrings, silver earrings that the house wore when it was ready to get married, and when I looked closer, I saw that she wore earrings that were miniature meat hooks, that her ears were made of mutton.

She liked to point up at the sky and slice it apart with her fingertip, naming each cut of the blue: rump, ribs, hock, hoof.

Sometimes she would say, *The sun is a meatball*, and I would joke by replying, *And what is the daughter*, and she would look at me and say, *The daughter is a cutting board*.

One morning, my aunts found the third widow hanging from the meat hooks, the flesh of her shoulders balled into fists around the hooks, her feet sparking against the ground, and when my aunts tore her down, we saw that her mouth was open and her teeth were deleted, and when they buried her in the cemetery up on the hills, my aunts said the third widow was never going to reincarnate, because she was buried un-whole, and that she would forever search our house for her teeth.

The fourth widow was younger than me.

As a child, she had been betrothed to another child, but the other child died of rain in the lungs and she outgrew him.

The fourth widow knew how to eat glass and showed me by licking down a lightbulb like a lollipop, dissolving it to syrup, her tongue adopting its coil of light, a light we could see even when her mouth was closed, a light all moths flocked toward.

When I tried to do the same, I was too impatient and bit down on the bulb, shards shrapneling my tongue, and when my aunts found out, they evicted the fourth widow, who ate the rest of our lightbulbs out of spite, so that that night when we turned on all our lights, the house stayed the color of our mouths.

The fifth widow could brew tea out of anything: leaves from our trees, trash from the gutters, newspaper, pages of the Bible, toenails.

This tea will make you holy, she said, while boiling pages of hymns in hot water, telling me to sip slow, to sing each word before I swallowed.

Once, she offered to cut my hair, and the next morning she was in our kitchen stewing the strands into ink, telling me to drink, and when I took a sip, I could taste everything that had ever touched my head, rain, my aunt's sweat, the sky, light.

The sixth widow was hairless and wore a silk scarf she'd bought a decade ago in Xi'an, a blue scarf that looked like the surface of a swimming pool, wired with light.

She told us that she had no hair because years ago she'd fallen into a dream, a dream about being an anglerfish in an ocean that was upside down, like the sky, and growing out of the top of her head was a lantern that lit her way.

She'd been dreaming so deep, her husband thought she had died and sent her away to be cremated, but the crematorium was unable to burn her body, possibly because she was composed of metal and glass, her body orchestrated from air.

The only part of her that burned was her hair, which never grew back, and her husband died a year after her failed cremation, having been hit in the head by a falling beam at a construction site for a mall in Orange County that imposed a dress code on its shoppers: no sweatpants, no T-shirts, only dresses and heels. After his death, she wore only dresses and heels, even to sleep, and at night we heard her walking up the stairs of the basement, calling to her husband to look up look up look up.

. . .

The seventh widow was a tailor who walked around the house with a pair of scissors, trimming and re-hemming the curtains, sewing my sleeves tighter around the wrist while I ate, her needles like insect legs, scuttling around the room when she didn't hold on to them.

My mother brought her wedding dress to the tailoring widow, asked the woman to let it out so that I could wear it when I was grown, but the tailoring widow looked at the dress—red, collared—and then at me and said, *This one won't wear a dress.*

I wanted to be the boys in the neighboring house, with their hair done blunt as blades, the way they whetted their legs on everything, the way their sweat dried into rust, and I wanted to run with them as they chased the girls and grabbed at their skirts like reins and yanked—

The girls chased them back, chased the boys with branches found on the street, threatening to shove them up their butts until the branches broke inside them and quilled the insides of their bladders, which was not anatomically correct, and nobody cared, and I was the one who kept changing sides, who kept going back and forth between being a girl and being a boy, who decided finally on being a shadow.

Impersonating shadows, I had to run as close as possible to the boy or the girl without their noticing—I had to imagine myself flat, like a night that had not yet been given legs, like a sea without any blue to buoy it.

The eighth widow was lucky at everything: lottery scratchers, slot machines, sons (she had seven of them, all of them living in the basement with her, though we didn't know until later).

The eighth widow lived off her luck and did not work; the eighth widow taught me to scratch at the lottery numbers with a penny and never my nails; the eighth widow taught me how to play blackjack; the eighth widow taught me the suits and what they meant: *King means husband, queen means wife, spade is the shovel she buries him with.*

Every week, the eighth widow snuck another of her sons down into the basement: She told us she only had one, but every week we heard a new voice boiling out of the basement, and for weeks we thought the one son was speaking to himself, until one day we caught all seven of them in the kitchen, eating the oranges off our shrine, and my mother beat each of the boys with her back scratcher and told the eighth widow not to come back.

The eighth widow offered my mother one of her sons if she allowed the rest of them to stay, but my mother said, *I have a son already, it's just that my son is my daughter.*

We pray to a god who is a girl in some countries and a boy in others.

I am trying to become something called a resident alien, which means I will be related to my television screen, to all the movies about little green men with heads like testicles, to all the movies about octopi who swim the sky, to all the movies about giving birth to another species, a baby that cannonballs out of your chest and kills you for your name.

Sometimes I pretend the widows are aliens from different planets, that they each adhere to their own gravity, and that is why the ninth widow floats instead of walks, and my mother loves her best because she doesn't get our carpet dirty.

The floating widow has pigeons for feet, and she sits cross-legged in the basement and feeds them seeds, nuts, spools of thread, crickets, wads of mantou, hair, balls of newspaper that expand in their bellies and teach them the speech of politicians.

The floating widow's pigeon-feet are very politically active and shit only on gentrifiers in the neighborhood, such as the man who goes jogging even when it rains—when he looks up, the floating widow is clouding overhead, her pigeon-feet shitting into his mouth.

I prefer living in basements because there are never any windows, the floating widow says, *because my bird-feet will fly into windows and die, and then I'll have no way to leave or go anywhere.*

The tenth widow wanted to live in a tent in our yard instead of the basement, mainly because she was interested in moonwatching, which she told me was not the same as just looking at the moon—moonwatching was the process by which you wooed a woman down from her night perch.

To woo the moon, you first have to threaten to gouge it out of the sky.

This can be done with chopsticks, a fork, tongs, anything with an end.

When the moon begins to fold itself in fear, you reach your hand out and make a fist around it—quick—the way you catch a knife as it falls—

When the moon is your fist, you teach it who to hit, what to light alive, how to wring the milk out of a man and curdle it into a crescent.

When the tenth widow opens her fist, the moon scatters like a flock of moths.

My mother once told me that every moth is the soul of someone lost and that's why you're not supposed to kill them. That's why there are so many. All our clothes grow holes in the knees, the breasts. Our nipples stick out like snouts. In the closet, our clothes swing like sides of meat. The moths are light-carnivores. I try to catch them alive, to close my fist around their onioned bodies, but I end up crushing them. They blur into the dirt, shunned into dust.

The eleventh widow was not a widow—her husband was not dead but locked away in the correctional facility on 11th Street, and we only found out from the letters she wrote him, which were written in some kind of code that only the two of them could read.

Out of jealousy, my aunts burned the eleventh widow's letters before she could send them, but the eleventh widow had them all memorized, and the next morning they were written on our walls, a hundred synonyms for *husband*, all of them meaning *missing*.

My aunts said it was unfair for some people to own a language that could not be sold to others, a language as private as the blood inside our bodies.

When I asked the eleventh widow what her husband had gone away for, she said, *Beating me,* and when I asked her if she loved him and why, she turned away and continued writing on the walls.

She taught me how to write my name in her two-person

language, which was now marrowed inside the walls, which was now ours. At night, wind ribboned around the house and slid through the leak in the ceiling, learning the language inside our walls and teaching it to the birds.

The twelfth widow was pregnant and told me stories of how her mother-in-law tried to force her to abort the baby by swallowing paper clips, a whole box of paper clips, because the idea was that they would snag on the fetus and drag it out of her body.

My mother says: *Some mothers are fishhooks—they're shaped to raise you, raise you out of the water for slaughter.*

My mother's mother caught fish for a living and sometimes sent foam packages with frozen fish shipped internationally, and the fish never went bad, not even after so many days in the air, a miracle none of us tried to name.

The thirteenth widow once worked as a whalesong writer, said she wrote whalesongs and recorded them on her phone and replayed them for whales, who learned the lyrics and sang along and popularized her songs.

Half of the world's whalesongs are written by me, she said, claiming she'd spoken in whalesongs for the first half of her life, that her parents had found her in the belly of a whale, a baby like a tumor on its underside, and that some scuba diver must have made love to the whale and impregnated it.

Because we are far from whales, when the thirteenth widow sang, nothing came, only lizards from the gutters, only mosquitos from the trash creek, only professional whale watchers who believed we were harboring a whale in our basement.

Once, the basement flooded and my mother and aunts ran around the house with buckets, trying to scoop out the water faster than it could rise, and the thirteenth widow did not run from the flood.

She ducked her head under the water and swam down, and when the water finally drained out, warping the floors into mirrors and the walls into baloney, we could not find her, not even after we pulled the floorboards up to search.

The fourteenth widow taught me how to tie knots around my wrists and get out of them.

When I asked her what was the point of tying the knots in the first place if I was going to get out of them, she told me it was practice for being kidnapped.

The fourteenth widow had never been kidnapped, but she kept a manila folder with newspaper clips of kidnapped girls and what kinds of knots had been found at various crime scenes.

The knots, she said, *the knots are the only thing I can teach you to undo:*

One knot was around my ankles and I got out of it with my canines—she taught me to gnaw on bouncy balls for practice, to tune my jaw into a tiger's, to hide a razor blade in my cheek. *The next line of defense,* she told me, *is to ascend. For example, I have a cousin who's a cloud. One time, her son put his hands around her neck and all he could wring out was rain.*

The fifteenth widow stole my mother's jewelry, the jade bangles I once thought big enough to wear as collars, the wedding gold that was going to be my dowry, the rings we won at the arcade, plastic with a light embedded inside a fake jewel that only turned on if you bit down on it.

Months later, my uncle saw the fifteenth widow pawning all the jewelry in Reno, saw her with a man, and that's when we learned she wasn't a widow at all.

The sixteenth widow loved hummingbirds and hung a feeder in our yard, told me that her father had reincarnated into one and that was why she fed them, in case one of them was her father.

When I asked her how her father had died, she said, *Of thirst*, told me that some men who had mishandled their memories could no longer even recognize their own thirst, so you had to trick them into drinking by soaking slices of bread in water and hand-feeding them.

If we stood very still with our palms full of sugar water, the hummingbird would drink from our hands, and I could hear their wings dicing up the air, could see the red feathers flirting on their chests like blood from a slit throat.

The seventeenth widow worked for years as an exterminator, and in the summer when the ants came, she sealed the space between our walls and the floor with duct tape and sprayed down our whole house with what we later learned was her sweat.

The seventeenth widow told us her sweat was acidic, her spit too, and that was why she had dentures at the age of twenty-five: Her own spit had churned her teeth into foam, and she couldn't even swallow without searing her throat.

To dilute the acid in her spit, the seventeenth widow swigged from a smoothie of baking soda and water, said she was trying to become basic, said that the only time she had kissed a man, his molars dissolved and later his tongue required skin grafts from his ass.

One time I asked the seventeenth widow to spit in a jar for me.

I kept the jar beside my mattress, saw it light up in the night, her spit incandescent as the inside of an apple.

Later, I stirred a tablespoon of her viscous spit into my bathwater, wanting to know what it was like to burn, and when I got out of the shower I had no more hair anywhere and my mother saw me and said I'd gone bald as a peanut, bald as when I was born.

I sold her acidic spit to the girls at school as a form of body-hair remover, and when they asked what it was, where I had bought it from, I said it was imported from Japan and that the spit was the gel of a squeezed leaf, born from a tree that grew without a shadow.

The eighteenth widow broke in and stayed in the basement for two weeks before we found her uprooting our floorboards, claiming to be looking for gold that the previous owner of the house had left her.

Before this house was our house, it was a horse ranch.

Sometimes, if you stood outside the house and looked in, you could see saddles floating through the living room, never any horses attached to them.

Horses were butchered in the basement and hung on hooks, because their meat could be canned and resold as anything: dog food, luncheon loaf, steak.

·   ·   ·

The nineteenth widow told me that it was possible to bleach
your irises blue by looking at the sky too long, so that's what
we did together, skywatch, skylick, waiting for the blue to in-
filtrate our eyes and develop them into a doll's. At first, I didn't
want blue eyes, because they melted fast as ice, and it's impossible to see with only water in your sockets, but the nineteenth
widow said a girl with eyes the color of sky would be able to
read the weather early, see storms before they arrived, set loose
her limbs as lightning.

The twentieth widow had been a beauty-school friend of my
mother's, and she had eyes with white pupils, moving like
maggots.

     She said this meant she could see the dead—not only dead
people but the spirits of roadkill too, and wherever she went
she wept for them, the possums that we ran over while they
were pregnant, steamrolling the babies inside them into por-
ridge.

     When she slept in the basement, she could see the bodies of
horses hanging from the hooks, and she said she couldn't bear
it, seeing their hooves off the ground like that, galloping on air,
going nowhere.

     The twentieth widow was newly a widow: She said her
husband had died in a war, though she couldn't remember
which war, only that it was fought using weapons that were
wielded by the tongue—miniature knives and bullets that had
to be spat—and he finally died one night after biting off his
own tongue and releasing it alive in a river, where it became a
freshwater eel.

When I asked to see a photo of him, she pointed at her own face and said they'd looked alike, so alike that even her own parents believed her husband to be their son, though they had never had a son and still wanted one.

My mother had a son before she had me, but he was raised by my grandparents in another country, and sometimes he emailed us photos of himself in his military uniform, his smile pieced from shark teeth.

There was a man who lived on the train tracks who had once been in a war, and sometimes he liked to smoke with my mother and tell stories about a horse he had seen in the field where he was born: It was pregnant and dead, and when he slit open its belly to save the baby, a human toddler waddled out into the soil.

The twenty-first widow had three birthdays a year but wouldn't let us sing to her once.

She said that she'd been born three times: first as a cocoon, then as a moth bursting out of the cocoon, then as a child shrugging out of the exoskeleton.

When she lifted her arms above the kitchen sink to shave, moth wings unfurled from her armpits and tried to fly her away.

The twenty-second widow I was in love with.

She wore her hair in one braid that was long enough to belt around the city, and I liked to loop it around my waist and take it to bed, light it like a wick between my thighs.

One night she reeled in her braid, tugging me down into the dark of the basement, tutoring my tongue into subter-

ranean shapes, fish or fishhook. When she departed one day
to become a nun, she cut off her braid and left it hissing on
my bed.

The twenty-third widow grew pomelos the size of her ass,
teaching me how to skin off the rinds with my fingers so that
I could suck out the meat inside and swallow it bitter.

I planted the rinds in our yard and nothing grew, but all
the crows gathered around the rind-grave and buried themselves there.

In the spring, our tulips hatched and I dug up the crow-
bones, strung them into bracelets and wore them around my
wrists, ringing the bone-bells of my hands.

The twenty-fourth widow was a jeweler who taught me how
to tell fake pearls from real ones: by grinding my teeth against
them and feeling the grit of salt, the give of it—counterfeit
pearls, she said, are smooth, pirated by girls in factories under
the sea, factories where daughters are sanding their own teeth
into perfect spheres and selling them.

I held up my fist and ground my teeth against the knuckle-
bones, but they were smooth and not gritty, which must mean
I'm fictional.

The twenty-fifth and twenty-sixth widows were twins who
had been born three seconds apart, and sometimes they spoke
at the same time but in different languages, a way of confusing any interrogators or police officers. There was a rumor that
years ago they killed each other's husbands and ate the corpses

to erase all evidence, and just in case it was true, my mother demanded X-rays of their stomachs, which tattled on their contents: cutlery, stray cats, and bones too small to belong to any man.

The twin widows began weaving silk scarves around the hooks, knotting them again and again until they became cocoons dangling down from the ceiling, gnarled and pearl-round.

When they left, my mother tried cutting down the cocoons they'd knotted, but nothing could cut through their silk, not even garden shears, not even meat scissors.

The cocoons rotated on their own, scarfing the shadows around themselves, feeding on mold and sweat from the ceiling.

One day I walked down into the basement with a baseball bat and beat the cocoons until they ripened, unseaming to reveal women inside, all of them born widows, widows with translucent skin and eyes broad as palms, praying open.

I opened every window in the house and begged them to leave, told them they were finally free, but the widows never woke: They hung there in the dark, molting into wind, playing their bones like flutes.

Virginia Slims

Mrs. Ngai passed out cigarette ads in magazines, the pages gilded to reflect our faces. There were perfume ads at the back of each magazine, and we musked ourselves with the sample strips, rubbing them against our armpits while Mrs. Ngai turned on the projector and showed us slides of lungs that had been excavated from the bodies of smokers. Our uncles and brothers and cousins owned lungs like these, so we dreamed of them as meteors, crystallized fists that lunged out of our mouths and would someday orbit us as moons.

After a minute of silent observation, Mrs. Ngai projected pairs of nonsmoker lungs, buoyant as the wads of bubble gum stitched to the undersides of our desks. After the slideshow, we were supposed to look at the cigarette ads and practice saying no to them. Yasmine looked down at the Marlboro man astride a greased stallion, his left hand wielding a lasso, his cowboy hat cocked down over a shadow-sliced face. She lingered her lips on the ledges of his cheeks, whispered *no* into his left ear.

Xiaoyang's ad pictured a gold-dusted camel in the desert, dunes with arched backs, yellow lettering, a horizon shiny as a zipper, the sun with a cigarette in its cartoon mouth, smoking out a scum of clouds. Xiaoyang shouted *no* at the camel until his mouth slurred with sand.

Melon's ad was the only woman. The woman was blond in an impossible way, the color of candlelight, the color of margarine at room temperature, the color of Melon's kneecap that time she tripped on a curb and peeled it open, exposing the fat beneath the skin. Her eyes were blue and pretty as smashed glass. A black beauty mark punctuated her left cheek, a place to pause your finger over. Eyelashes curved up into sickle blades. Melon was felled by that face. The woman was lying on her side at the beach, wearing a white Marilyn Monroe dress with a neckline that rivaled the shoreline behind her, a peninsula of skin bared between her breasts. Sand speckled her calves and thighs. Melon could smell the pleats of salt between the woman's legs, the waves unfurling like tongues behind her, waiting to lick her onto her back. The woman's lips formed around the cigarette as if around a sound, a name made smoke. A speech bubble was tethered to her head and said: *You've come a long way, baby.* Melon wondered if this was what the sea was translating, if the woman in the ad had come as far as Melon's mother just to ask for a cigarette.

Melon's mother only told stories while she smoked, most of them beginning as warnings. *We would not,* her mother said, *be your ninth uncle on your father's side, the one who moved to Leshan and went to a salon to get his hair cut and woke up in a vegetable-fermentation tub without his kidneys. We would not be your biaoge, who snuck into other people's garages to sleep in their cars at night and died of inhaling something only cars could stomach, which at least was painless. We would not,* her mother said, *be like your fifth aunt Yangyang, who left for Na-gano without telling anyone and without a man, your aunt Yangyang, who cleaned hotel rooms for two years before she fi-nally jumped out of the seventeenth-floor window.* There were other warnings, but all Melon could think about was her fifth aunt in Nagano, who had been the best in the family at telling ghost stories. That aunt had had a baby, a Japanese baby, but none of them knew what kind of man he'd grown up to be, and besides, her mother said, he was different: He would die where he was born and live in one body his whole life. He would never become a ghost in a story. A ghost had no body to come back to.

Melon remembers this story told by her aunt Yangyang: Once, there was a woman who migrated back from the dead to the living. She traveled like smoke, sifted into houses and cleaned them with her steam-breath. But everything that the ghost touched grew spines overnight: When the owners went to bed that evening, their mattresses sprouted three-foot thorns and skewered them while they slept. After that, everyone in the city feared coming home to a clean house, knowing that a ghost woman had been there, perforating table legs into bone marrow, coaxing crops of knives up from the carpet.

The last slide of the anti-smoking presentation was of a lung being blown up like a bicycle tire, pumped until it burst. We all ducked under the desk to avoid the splatter. *Each of us has a capacity for air*, Mrs. Ngai said. *How much you are able to carry will depend on your habits and your family history.* After the slideshow and after we rehearsed saying *no* at least three times more, we had to give our ads back. But Melon folded hers and tucked it into her fist, sliding it into her pants. We said nothing of her theft. At home, she flattened out the ad with her hands and asked the blond woman her name, trying to speak in sync with the sea behind her. The woman said her name was Virginia. *What kind of name is Virginia*, Melon said. *Only old women are named that.* Virginia said, *Do I look old to you?* and Melon said no. *What kind of name is Melon*, Virginia said, and Melon said, *Mine.* Virginia didn't move her mouth to speak: The cigarette behaved like a beak, twitching up and down between her lips, wand-like, casting smoke like a spell. Melon wanted to pry Virginia's jaw open with her fingers, but Virginia cinched her lips around the cigarette, mouth tight as an asterisk. Melon's thumb flicked the page, jarring ash off the tip of Virginia's cigarette. Melon asked Virginia to call her *Baby*, and Virginia did, tongue lapping at the center seam of the page.

Melon touched the page, stroking the lard-blond of Virginia's hair. She decided that Virginia must be wearing a wig, that she must really be Chinese, because only Chinese girls had old white-lady names—she knew a girl named Gloria who everyone else called Gloryhole, because she had a tendency to fall asleep in class with her mouth wide open, and it was Gloria who once called Melon an anchor baby, not because any of them knew what it meant but because it sounded endearing: *baby* as in baobei. The way Virginia said *baby* was different: Somehow she made every word sound like want.

Melon folded Virginia into fourths and slid the ad under her pillow. In the morning, Virginia migrated off the page and was sitting on the corner of Melon's bed, a seam of shadow down the center of her face where Melon had made a crease. Virginia was taller than Melon but two-dimensional, pasting herself to the wall like a good-luck charm. Melon peeled Virginia off the plaster, unfurled her on the carpet, and stood on Virginia's paper-flat belly, pinning her silhouette to the floor. Virginia blinked up at her and smiled, her eyes sculpted from

seagull droppings. Melon no longer remembered why she'd
wanted to take Virginia home, if it was because Virginia looked
like the same species as the sea (salted and free), or if she
wanted to know who Virginia was looking at, reclined on the
beach as if the world was her skirt, its hem within reach.
Melon wanted to be the thing Virginia was looking at. She
wanted to be Virginia's only window. But now Virginia was
creased and crumpled against the carpet, looking up at Melon
with the stillness of a stone fruit. She remembered something
her aunt in Nagano once told her over the phone before she
died, that telling lies will hollow out your bones, and if you tell
enough of them you'll float. When she looked down at Virginia, Melon lied and said, *I want you to leave, please.*

Virginia was silent, the cigarette in her mouth shedding
swarms of ash that buzzed like fireflies. Melon batted the ash
away from her face, and Virginia's unmoving mouth repeated
the same line over and over again, the one lassoed inside her
speech bubble: *You've come a long way, baby.*

Actually, Melon said, *I was born here.* Another lie. Virginia
smiled, her teeth as far away as stars. *Don't you recognize me?*
Virginia said, and rolled her eyes upward. Melon squinted and
saw that Virginia's hairline, which yesterday had been as dis-
tinct as a sand-gold shoreline, was now shadowed. Her hair
was black at the roots. *No,* Melon said. *I don't know anybody
with your name.* Virginia's mouth cinched tighter, strangling
the butt of her cigarette, which was now dull and stumped.
*I've lied so many times in my lifetime that my bones are paper
now,* Virginia said. Melon paused, stepping off Virginia's torn
torso. Wafting upward, Virginia floated upright and clung to
the far wall of the bedroom.

Ayi? Melon said. *Are you my ayi?* Virginia said nothing, a
crease cleaving her face. Melon peeled Virginia off the wall

and tried smoothing her out with her palms, but Virginia said nothing, not even when Melon reached out and scratched Virginia's cheek with her fingertip, skinning the ink from the page. *I'm sorry, Yangyang Ayi,* Melon said, shielding the scar with her thumb. *I just want to ask you where you've been.* Virginia was silent again until after school, when Melon walked home and unfurled Virginia from under the bed. *You've come a long way, baby.* It began to sound like a taunt, a prayer.

Melon's bedroom doubled as a wig storage room, the place where her mother sewed costume wigs to sell online, her latest in a series of failing businesses. She dyed them every color of the sky, and Melon's room was a museum of faceless mannequin heads, each wearing a wig that resembled a half-plucked chicken or acid rain.

In her room, Melon slit her scissors along Virginia's hairline, trying to expose her aunt's hair beneath. Before she'd moved to Japan, her aunt Yangyang sold all her hair to a wigmaker in Yilan. She called Melon's mother and wept into the phone, saying that her hair was once so long that the local men crawled under it to sleep. *She should be glad her hair is the virgin kind,* Melon's mother said. *Everyone wants the virgin stuff. That's what they pay for.* When Melon asked what virgin hair was, her mother said, *It's hair that's never been dyed before.* What Melon heard was *hair that's never died before.* Melon asked, *Isn't all hair already dead?* and her mother said, *Yes, hair is dead; that's why it never hurts you to sever it.*

Every month, Melon's mother sat her on the rim of the bathtub and cut her hair, trimming the ends with kitchen scissors. The month her aunt Yangyang died, Melon's mother cut her hair close to the nape, snipping with the speed of teeth, one of the blades fanging into her neck. Melon bled in handfuls of garnets, and when she yelped and turned around, pressing her palm to the wound, she saw her mother standing with the scissors in her hands, silent and still. For a moment, Melon wondered whether her mother had done it on purpose, cutting her like that, but before she could ask, her mother rushed forward with a towel in her hand, stanching the wound with both hands, the scissors dropped into the bathtub, *sorry sorry sorry.* Later that same month, Melon stole her mother's lighter and brought the tip of the flame to her hair, singeing the ends blue. There was a part of her that believed she could coerce her hair into feeling.

They burned paper money on the anniversary of her aunt Yangyang's death, money with the king of hell printed on it, a bribe for demons. Melon's aunt was cremated and shelved somewhere anonymously. *There's a practice,* Melon's mother said, *that we learned from the Japanese. You bury the body, and after seven years, you dig up the grave and pluck the bones out of the hole with a pair of long chopsticks. One by one. That's what we did to our mother, your aunt Yangyang and I. The bones were so empty they almost floated out.* Melon's mother mimed bone-picking with her fingers, but her fingers looked more like scissors, severing rather than saving.

After a week of Virginia's silence, Melon attempted to paste back the cut-out shreds of her blond hair, which Melon began to suspect was dyed, no longer virgin. When she still didn't speak, Melon cut Virginia's mouth into a hand-sized hole so that it would be easier for her aunt to shuttle sound through it, but the result was that Virginia no longer spoke at all. Her mouth said nothing but shade. At night, Melon held Virginia up to her window, aligning her body so that the moon shone through the hole of her mouth. She could pretend that

light was language. *If it's really you, Yangyang Ayi*, Melon
said, *tell me a ghost story.* Virginia's face was wrinkled from
the weight of Melon's pillow, her face etched like the map of
another continent, borderlines and roads and rivers that Melon
couldn't follow. Silence replaced Virginia's skin, sequinning
the air like heat haze. That night, when Melon was sitting
between her mother's knees for her haircut, she asked, *Was
Ayi's hair still a virgin when she died?* Her mother set down the
scissors on the edge of the tub, the ceramic chipped like teeth.
She had a baby, her mother said, *but I don't know what happened to him. He's one of them now.* Melon shut her eyes and
imagined Virginia's Marilyn Monroe gown blown up like a
parachute, a baby strapped into the space between her thighs.

That night, after plucking strands of black hair out of the
shower drain with a pair of chopsticks, Melon spread Virginia
out on the bed. Above her, mannequin heads swung on hooks,
mimicking the moon. She flicked on the lighter stolen from
her mother and remembered the paper money, the hell king's
face bearded in flames. There were stores downtown that sold
miniature paper people, men with hats like propeller blades
and women in paper gowns painted with interlocking birds,
fighting or flying. Melon always believed the paper people
were burned alive so that the dead could have friends, but
Melon's mother said they were servants who would cook and
clean for you, and Melon prayed that her aunt was not cleaning up after anyone in the afterlife, that she was in a country
where the clouds came down to mop the ground.

In the dark, Virginia's white dress spanned the bed like a
shroud. Melon ironed out the creases in Virginia's dress with
her elbows and knees. Propping up Virginia's paper face,
Melon reached her hand through the empty hole of Virginia's
mouth, making a fist in place of sound. Then she flicked on

her mother's lighter and fed fistfuls of Virginia to the flame, ash sprinkling down like seed, planting deep. The bedsheets were a field of fire, burning fast as paper. Melon fled the bed, opening every window for the smoke to migrate out and calcify in the sky, slender and white as a bone plucked alive from the hole of night.

Mariela

Mariela had a brother made of ash. She showed me a picture of him, down in that soft-boned basement where the ceiling perched on your head and where Mariela's parents slept with their bodies pointing in opposite directions. Her mother always sleeping with her head at the foot of the bed to confuse demons. Her father sleeping with a BB gun cupped in his right hand like a hard-on.

Mariela showed me a photo album that was slotted between the wall and the nightstand where her father kept his gold rings, flattened packs of cigarettes, and a medal he'd gotten from the military. The picture in the album was of a baby with the dirt-darned face of a tulip bulb. The baby's hands were both fists, and around its neck was a gold cross. Jesus side-eyeing the wounds on his palms. The necklace must have been a bracelet, to fit like that around his splinter-thick baby neck. When I asked where he was, Mariela said, *7-Eleven*, but she must have meant *heaven*.

I mean where's his body, I said. *Where's he buried?* Mariela
said he was boiled inside his mother like a yam and then born
into an urn and that one night she found her mother sitting in
the bathroom. In the dark, her mother was squatting there on
the tiles, scooping handfuls of ash into her mouth, dust fur-
ring the floor. She sat embalmed in the night, as if staying still
was something you could be sainted for. Mariela backed out
and shut the door, and in the morning, the urn was gone and
her mother's mouth was wiped clean of all sound. Her mother
stopped speaking. Now she could only make two sounds, one
like a broken-winged crow and another like a door hinge severing a pinky.

Mariela said she wanted to tie a bell around her mother's
neck, the way you do with cows so you know where they are,
and I told her that cows are bred for killing and grilling and
that no one should be collared that way. But Mariela said it
wasn't so bad, being belled: When she was little, her mother
tied strings of safety pins around her ankles so that they would
shimmy into song whenever she walked. She followed Mariela
from room to room, roofing her daughter with her shadow,
keeping her away from anything sharp. *I grew up in her dark,*
Mariela told me, *just like my brother, who's living in an urn.* I
told her that we could let in a little light by prying open the
urn lid, but Mariela said no one was allowed to touch it. *Look,*
she said, crawling under the bed, and I ducked into the dark
with her: The urn was squatting there, round and brassy as a
bell, and I wondered if it would make a sound if we struck it,
if its song would show us where he was.

In the basement, Mariela put the photo album away, and
we went back upstairs to watch the blue jays brawl themselves
bald, but for weeks I woke at home and saw the baby's eyes

open on my ceiling, unzipping to reveal teeth. The baby's eyes were two mini-mouths, and I knew then that it was a hungryghost, the kind my mother told me to pray against. She would tell me it was bad luck and very sick, keeping ashes inside your home, like trying to keep a baby forever in your belly. I didn't know anyone dead until Mariela. Mariela was the one who stretched my memory like a collar to accommodate other bodies, other pasts.

Our favorite game was to dangle upside down on the monkey bars and pretend the tanbark was our sky and the sky was at our feet. We dangled side by side and held hands and all our blood bent at the knees, rose upstream to our heads. I turned redder because I was lighter-skinned, and she laughed at how I looked, my hair flipped upside down like an umbrella in a storm. I kissed her open mouth, snagging my lips on the whites of her teeth. She jerked away and our knees straightened and we fell on our faces, a piece of tanbark piercing a hole through my cheek that my mother had to stitch up with mint-glossed floss. Mariela chipped her canine tooth, which fell out the next week, leaving behind a hole big enough for the sun to steal into her mouth.

When her gums stopped bleeding and my cheek hole was sewn closed, we kissed right side up. A sequin of my spit on the corner of her lip. This time, my blood rowed downstream, and when she put her fist inside my hand-me-down shorts that stank of boy-sweat, I clutched her wrist between my thighs. My tongue prodded the loose baby tooth at the back of her mouth. It popped from the socket and slipped into my cheek. Mariela pulled her head back and grabbed my face, trying to squeeze it out of me, but I swallowed. It caught in my throat and rang like a bell when I breathed. *You owe me a tooth,* she told me, but there was pleasure in being indebted to her. Later she told me there were two types of kisses in the world, the boyfriend kiss and the wedding kiss. The boyfriend kiss was mouth-to-mouth. The wedding kiss was mouth-to-where-you-pee, and I wasn't allowed to tell anyone we did it.

Mariela told me we'd antelope. I said, *Don't you mean elope? An antelope is an animal,* I said, and Mariela smiled at me, her missing baby teeth like a piano's minor keys. She said, *You're the animal,* and then she rolled with me on the playground. I called Mariela my antelope, told her I'd hunt her down someday and mount her on a wall if she wouldn't marry me. Our wedding would happen at sea, I told her, and there would be no ash brothers or basements. We would be married on a glass boat, transparent so that we could look down and see straight to the bottom of the ocean, where all the fish swam on their sides and the whales made love to each other's blowholes.

We decided to antelope in June, when it wasn't yet hot enough for our bones to soften and disband. It was my first secret: that Mariela and I were going to become animals, that the gold wedding bangles my mother kept in a duct-taped kitchen drawer—preparation for when it was time for me to marry a man—were never going to be worn by anybody. Sometimes I saw my mother un-tape the drawer and look in, her face lamped by the gold inside, and she'd unsheathe an earring from its velvet pouch and hold it up to my ear, tell me it matched the color of my surname. I didn't remember when all her sentences began to taper into the same one, the one that began, *When you have a husband,* but now I had an antelope—a girl who sat on my back in the playground and pretended to gallop me.

.   .   .

On the last day of fifth grade, Mariela and I sat in the parking lot, waiting for her mother to come pick her up. I'd only ever seen Mariela's mother through the car window: When she dropped Mariela off in the mornings, she pressed her elbow to the horn and waved at me, her left arm rattling with lacquered bangles. Sometimes, Mariela and I tried to get her to call for help by pretending to have simultaneous strokes. We convulsed and fell to the ground, me clutching my chest and Mariela clutching her head, because we couldn't decide where in the body a stroke happened. But her mother never shouted or said anything, just pulled up to the curb and honked again as we seized on the sidewalk, trying to die identically.

While we waited for her mother, Mariela plucked out the stray hairs on her calves, needling her nails into the skin. I knew she was waxing them with duct tape, but when I tried to do the same, I was too afraid to tear the tape from my skin, and the strips wilted away in my sweat. Mariela said she had a new game: We each had to choose the other's best feature and let the other girl wear it. I asked how this was possible, and she said, *You choose first.* Sweat made her skin shine like flypaper: Touching her was a trap. I looked at her hair instead, her dandruff like dehydrated light. I always thought it was pretty that she could precipitate wherever she walked. *You're taking too long,* she said, *I'll go.* I waited for Mariela to choose something I was willing to part with, and after a few seconds she said, *Your eyelashes.*

Okay, I said, and shut my left eye, closing my fingers on the fringe of my lashes and tugging until it tore away, my eye lining itself in blood. She opened her hand and I gave her the fan of my lashes, some skin still on them. *There are still some left*, Mariela said, pointing at my eye, *but this is enough for me to grow my own*. She'd put them in water, she explained, until she had enough of my eyelashes to replace hers. *Your turn*, she said. I figured her face into a math equation, adding her mouth to my eyes, her cheeks to my chin. But I couldn't imagine the sum.

Your teeth, I said, testing her. When she smiled, two of her bottom teeth overlapped, angled to joust each other. She looked down at the sidewalk where we sat. *Okay*, she said, *watch*.

Kneeling in the gutter, Mariela lifted her head and slammed her face into the curb. When she looked up, her bottom lip was torn open, raw inside as a slug, and there was a molar on the ground. Blood threaded through her spit, a red chain tugging her chin to the pavement. Mariela's mother pulled up to us in her car and opened her mouth, but there was no sound that could match this scene, and through the car window her mouth was cartoon-wide, a letter O typed onto her face. I took the tooth from the sidewalk and folded it into my fist.

Mariela's mother got out of the car and hoisted her into the backseat by the armpits, slamming the door. As they pulled away, Mariela pressed her face to the passenger window and laughed, but I couldn't hear anything. The tooth tucked itself deep inside my skin like a seed, planted itself there. Her mouth in my hands. When I prayed at night, it was my hand that I addressed: My palm grew a sheath of skin over the molar, disguising the bump as a callus or a scar. When I touched myself with that hand, a toothache hummed in the center of my palm.

My mother won tickets to Raging Waters from a raffle at the Taiwanese First Presbyterian Church, where she cleaned the basement and translated pamphlets and lied about being a believer and where, most importantly, the food was free every weekend. *Don't waste free things,* my mother said. *Eat so much you won't be hungry for a hundred years.* We called this kangarooing, and I wished I could slit my belly open and fan out the food inside me, lengthening it like an accordion, the sheets of rippling beef, the fat I fingered into wicks.

When I invited Mariela to come to the water park with me, she told me that her mother had pointed at the headline of a news story about a girl who fell off the top of a waterslide and burst like a watermelon. She grasped Mariela's elbows and shook her head, refusing to leave the house, so Mariela's father took us instead. He arrived in an SUV slick as dog slobber. We pushed down the fake-leather seats and lay down side by side, staring at the felt ceiling constellated with cigarette burns. Her father claimed he'd quit smoking, but he reached for a lighter duct-taped under his seat and smoked out the window as we drove.

Mariela's favorite waterslide was the Great White Shark. It was a gray tube that entered the mouth of a shark, its teeth neon and mossed at the tips, and when the inner tube was swallowed inside it, the shark's ribs lit up, red lights embedded like the freckles that breaded white girls' breasts. We slicked out of the shark and into another gray tube that shat us out into a shallow pool. We liked to use the two-person inner tube, the kind that looked like two donuts stitched together, and we always made sure to lay on our backs and not on our bellies the way teenagers did, mostly because we wanted to look up at the rubied ribs of the shark and a little bit because we'd heard a story about a boy who went down on his belly and his penis snagged on the plastic seam between two pieces of the slide and it broke off and no one could find it, though some say it reemerged in the fake tidal pool, where it brushed the cheek of someone's mother and had to be ladled out by the fake lifeguard and strangled in a plastic bag.

We shunted into the shark's mouth again and again, its hollow belly glossed with pink slime, and I wondered how many church meals could be swallowed inside it. When the line into the shark's mouth got too long, we went to the fake tidal pool and tried to sneak into the deep end, except the fake lifeguard with his foam ring pointed at the height chart and said we couldn't, since the fake waves might yank us down like reins, and since he himself was fake, he could not rescue us from the sea, and so we stood in line for chili dogs instead. We couldn't buy chili dogs, since they were four dollars each and my mother had packed us leftover church meat, some kind of pork with a salt-hardened sauce, but we liked to wait in line wet and in our two-pieces because we thought the boys would look at us.

Are they looking at us yet? we asked each other, but there were only mothers in line, and the boys who did look at us had their hands cradling their crotches, probably thinking about the story of the boy who went down on his belly, so we went back in line for the shark. While we were climbing up together, Mariela told me what a blow job was. We were carrying the inner tube on our shoulders and pretending to be pallbearers. I told her I didn't believe her, that there was no way it went inside your mouth. There was only room in the mouth for a language or two. Mariela said no, it was true, it went in your mouth and it was called a blow job, and I thought she meant *blow* as in literally: You pumped it up the way you inflated a balloon animal, and then you could pretzel-twist it into any shape you wanted. *Why in the mouth?* I asked her. Mariela said that mouths are like vaginas, except with better technology. *Mouths have teeth,* Mariela explained, *so you can bite down on the baby he tries to put in you, which you cannot do down-there.*

At the top of the slide, the white boy held down our inner tube so that we could get on, and I sat first. Mariela sat in front of me, braiding my legs around her waist, and when the boy leaned forward to push us through the jaw of the tunnel, she reached up and grabbed the front of his swim trunks, twisting his crotch in her fist. The boy yelped and fell to his knees, letting go. We slicked down the throat of the tunnel, my hands gripping Mariela's hair, haltering her head, laughing while I tried not to open my mouth, because my mother said the water here was embroidered with bacteria and if I swallowed any she'd punch my belly until I gagged it back out. When I turned my head back, the boy was still crouched, his hands cupping his crotch. I asked her later why she did that, and Mariela laughed. She said he probably liked it, that he'd been eyeing our belly buttons like coin slots in a vending machine.

We got in line again, and Mariela swiveled around to face me, saying that boys only ever wanted to look at the backside of things. I liked it better when she faced me, when I could see her mouth, that pearl-sized protrusion in her upper lip that my mother said meant she could talk her way out of being born, the pearl I tried to make of my own mouth by biting off the tip of my lip, letting it dangle like a pink peninsula. Mariela explained to me about anatomy, how the shark was incorrect—*it's totally empty inside, where's the heart, the stomach*—and I wanted to say, *The shark is dead, it's only empty so we can enter it.* But I didn't say anything else, about how my favorite part of its body was the outing, all the organs evacuating so the dark could digest us entirely, and this way, when she leaned her head back between my legs to look up at the ribs, I could look down at her face for as long as I wanted, as long as my life. Then the light lassoed us out again and we were in the water, blinking like we'd just been born.

At the beginning of sixth grade, Mariela's mother avoided all light. She drove with insect screens over the windows, the sun caught dead in their mesh. Mariela said her mother could take both of us home, but I think she was afraid of riding in the dark alone. *It's called carpool*, Mariela said, which made me excited at first because I thought it meant the car would be filled with water and we'd have to hold our breaths the whole way home. But Mariela's mother did not arrive with water: She came with tinfoil-wrapped pork-floss sandwiches and a pair of sunglasses that lidded half her face in shadow. She wore a tie-dye jacket with a hood, a jacket I recognized as belonging to Mariela, and I wondered when she and her mother had become the same size, if it was Mariela who was growing or if her mother was the one shrinking. When I asked Mariela what had happened to her mother, Mariela told me that she'd gotten eye surgery, which my mother later told me was what you needed when your eyes were bad and needed to be fixed, though I'd never seen Mariela's mother wear any kind of glasses before.

The week after that, when her mother picked us up wearing a different pair of sunglasses—this time the kind with star-shaped frames you could get at the dollar store—Mariela told me she'd gone to Taiwan to get discount plastic surgery. The surgeons had sucked the fat from her under-eye bags so that she'd never look tired again. In the car, I asked how it was possible for her to fly to Taiwan and get the fat sucked out of her eyelids and then fly back in time to pick us up, but Mari-

ela's mother didn't speak and Mariela adopted the silence as
her own. At the stoplight, Mariela's mother adjusted the scarf
around her neck. The windows were down and the wind un-
knotted it, teasing the tassels at the end. Where the fabric
lifted from her neck, I saw the shadow of something branched,
a tree maybe, something rooted in her throat that was prepar-
ing to grow out of her mouth.

Mariela saw me watching her mother and leaned forward,
punching the back of the driver's seat with both her fists.
When she wanted to, Mariela knew how to hurt. How to take
any word out of the air and reroute it through her own mouth,
distorting its meaning. Once, on the playground, she'd taken
my hair in her hands and wrapped her fists in it, tugging so
gently I almost kneeled in front of her. When I began to lower
myself, she yanked up with her hands and tore out a handful
of my hair.

Speak, Mariela said to her mother. It was the same way
we'd spoken to each other when we played Dog in elementary
school, a game we both pretended to outgrow. To play Dog,
one of us had to be the dog, and the other had to give orders. I
liked the feeling of a branch in my mouth, the splinters I
plucked out of my gums later, the tang of soil and rain. I liked
her hand down my back, the way she scratched my bare belly
hard enough to bleed. There were other commands I liked
less, like being told to sit or speak or eat whatever she held out
in her palms. Sometimes we were both the dog, and we ran
around the blacktop drinking directly from puddles, lapping at
water that was beaded with mosquito eggs.

Mariela's mother pressed the gas pedal and sped forward.
The insect screens were whisked off the windows. She drove
past the 7-Eleven and past the trash creek where an unidenti-
fied boy had once been pulled from the water and past the car

wash with the broken popcorn machine and past the grocery
where Mariela and I plucked crumpled-up lottery scratchers
out of the trash, looking for a winning ticket that had been
missed. Mariela's mother sped faster, until each corner con-
tracted and expanded and the sycamores along the street became conjoined twins, each of their branches a shared limb.

Mariela kicked and punched the back of her mother's seat,
saying, *Speak Speak Speak*, until it was a chant, and when
Mariela's mother finally stopped, I looked out the window and
saw that we were at their duplex. The car door unlocked and
Mariela's mother got out, the end of her scarf grasped in one
fist. She pulled Mariela out of the backseat. Mariela's face was
the color of a newborn's, blue-purple and scrunched, and she
was tearing the stuffing out of a slit in the car seat, lobbing it
at her mother. *Say something*, Mariela said, as she landed on
her back on the street and was dragged by the arms all the way
to the sidewalk.

Mariela continued to scream, the radius of her voice ex-
panding like a water ring. I watched her from the passenger
seat, leaning away from the window as if her voice might claw
me. We left her behind. Her mother turned away, got back
into the car, and pulled away so fast I heard the wheels wail.
I'm sorry, I said, though I wasn't sure what I was sorry for or if
I was saying it to Mariela or her mother.

She drove slowly now, turning onto a side street I didn't
recognize, flanked by a junkyard with cars stacked like coffins,
the front windshields shattered where their drivers must have
hit the glass, flung forward by the force of impact. Mariela's
mother was not wearing her seatbelt, and I watched her
through the rearview mirror. At any moment, I thought, she
might let go of the wheel. I had never looked at her face closely
before, and now I could only see the crest of one cheekbone,

where her glasses cast their shadow. She had dimples. When I tried to remember what her eyes looked like before the sunglasses, I could only see the urn, the copper one with her son's ashes, engraved like a turtle's back, too elaborate to be manmade. Down in that basement, when I reached out to touch it before Mariela slapped my hand away, I heard it hum with heat, as if something still beat alive inside it.

When we got to my street, the one with the train tracks and the old factory converted into a dog pound, where sometimes they put down the dogs and incinerated their bodies in an oven at night so that no one could see the smoke in the dark, Mariela's mother pulled up to the curb and idled, breathing hard. She watched me through the rearview mirror, and because it felt wrong when my own face was so exposed and hers was shielded, I got out of the car and left without saying goodbye. I ran to the back unit of the duplex and let myself in with the key my mother gave me—she told me to never let anyone take it from me, to swallow it before anyone could steal it—and looked at my face in the bathroom mirror. Pinched at the skin beneath my eyes, imagined the pearling fat inside. When my mother came home smelling of bleach, I didn't tell her about Mariela's mother, the scarf and the glasses, the sandpapered silence of the car ride. Instead, I tested how long I could go without speaking, how well I could thread silence down my own throat, but it ended as soon as my mother said my name.

That was the year Mariela's mother began to hum. Mariela told me it began at night, in the bathroom where she'd once squatted and eaten ash. One night, Mariela woke up and heard a humming in the walls, a humming that emptied her bones, and so she followed the sound to the bathroom. The door was shut, and when she opened it, her mother was splayed on her back, sound rising off her. Mariela kneeled and saw that her mother's eyes were open too, and when she turned on the lights, her mother sat up and stuck out her tongue, filtering the sound into a higher hum. Like acid lights. Like a mosquito amplified in the arena of your ear.

Mariela's mother walked back to bed, but she wouldn't stop humming, not even when her husband plugged a sock in her mouth. Unable to sleep, Mariela's father climbed up the basement stairs and slept in the kitchen, on the tiled floor, his sweat flooding the cracks. In the morning, when her mother's hum only grew louder, almost symphonic, Mariela tried to seal her mother's mouth with a strip of duct tape, but the humming was born not from the mouth but from some subterranean source, the belly or the bowels, and so the tape did nothing but accessorize her.

I couldn't sleep at all, Mariela told me at school. The skin under her eyes was blue. I told her she should get that surgery her mother got, the one that sucked the fat out from under your eyes, and Mariela told me to shut up. We were between class periods, and she asked me to help her find a way to fix her mother's humming. The neighbors had already called an exterminator. Mariela's father lied and said it was a plumbing problem, possibly an electrical problem. *She's in the basement now,* Mariela said. *I think he locked her in there. We have to take the bus home today,* she said, *or walk.*

I thought of her mother in the basement, shadows circling her face like birds. *We should let her out,* I said. Mariela looked at me, elbowed me in the chest. She said I didn't know her mother. I didn't know what kind of sound she made, how it hurt to hear.

We walked home after school. Mariela held my hand and asked if I remembered how we used to play Dog. *Of course,* I said, remembering my hair in her hands, her fingers thrumming the strands. *Walk*, she said, and squeezed my hand. I ran.

On her block, we passed the foot spa with the prices written directly on the window in red marker and crossed the street to her duplex. There was a separate door to the basement and stairs that only seemed solid if you tiptoed, playing each stair like a piano key, descending notes all the way down. The ceiling had lowered since Mariela last let me in to show me her brother. When I looked up, I saw leaks as intricate as arteries.

I followed Mariela into the dim, the carpet damp and freckled with mold. Mariela's mother was lying on the bed, her bare legs planked out. I was embarrassed by how much hair was on them, thick as a shroud draped over her knees. She sat up when we approached. I didn't hear the humming until I saw her, and then it was an impossible sound, a humming that seemed to surround us, to come from nowhere, wrung from the rag of the ceiling.

She wasn't wearing her glasses, and one of her eyes looked like it'd been sewn shut, cauterized. *Stop it*, Mariela said, lunging forward. *Stop, stop.* In the dark, I could see the stray hairs on Mariela's calves, the stubborn ones she bleached into wicks and lit. Mariela's hand sailed forward, hit her mother's face. Her mother did not flinch. She opened her mouth and I looked into it, counting the chipped bunkers of her molars, and Mariela rushed forward again, covering her mother's mouth with her hand. *Speak*, Mariela said, though she was holding her mother's face motionless. I tried to pry away Mariela's hands, but they were magnetized to her mother's skin. Outside, I could hear the stars hit the roof like rain. Mariela's mother kept humming, a low note like the beginning of a ballad. It reminded me of a story my mother told me once, about how she and Mariela's mother used to work together at a pearl factory. *It was years ago*, my mother said, *and she was good at scouring*. A pearl is born round or oval or flat, and you're not supposed to change what it is. But she wanted to decide its shape. *She could make a sphere so perfect you could turn it and turn it in your fingers like a little globe. You could be anywhere in that light.* I looked at her lap now. Tried to imagine a world between her fingers.

Mariela reeled back and lunged forward again. I kneed her in the side, drilling into her ribs until she curled to the carpet. I wondered if she was the reason her mother did not speak. I was breathless, wasps in my chest, and Mariela's mother kept humming.

Mariela shoved me off, got up. She said something I couldn't hear over the humming, though I still remember the sickled shape her mouth made. She dropped to her stomach and slid under the bed while her mother hummed so deep, a pipe opened above us and spat water. Mariela shimmied back out from under the bed and stood before her mother. The urn in her hands, perched in her palms.

Eat it, Mariela said, bringing the urn to her mother. There were words carved on the urn, too shallow to read. The urn looked skinless, soft as an organ, and I reached forward to cradle it. But Mariela moved away from me, kneeling with the urn in front of her mother.

Her mother sat unseeing, still humming. *What was his name?* I said, thinking if she spoke, then Mariela would stop, Mariela would bury her brother back under the dark. But I knew I was asking the wrong thing. Mariela's mother reached forward, her hands palm-up like she was praying, taking the urn from her daughter's hands.

Eat it, eat it, Mariela said. Ash sputtered out of the urn, crumbing the carpet, and among the dull sand I could see bits of bright, a molar or a bead of bone, but when I tried to swipe it all away with my feet, Mariela pushed me to my knees. Her hands hooked into her own mouth, filling it with ash. And all around us the ash fluttered upward, pollinating the air, flocking out of the urn and into our ears, burying us where we knelt.

I saw Mariela's mother alone only once. It was night and it was summer and I didn't know yet about the dead brother. The windows of our duplex were open, moths clutching like scabs to my bedroom wall. I peeled them off my palms and tried herding them outside, but they scattered in the air like thrown salt. In the gape of the window, I saw a woman standing on the street, the blacktop bright as a scraped-open knee. She was looking up at a duplex, the one with the basement where I'd left my breath. It should've been impossible for me to see her neighborhood from here, unless my window was dilated wide as the sky, but I knew the woman was Mariela's mother. Silence shawled her, thickening her silhouette. I wondered why she was standing outside her own home. She was wearing the kind of nightgown I'd seen in old movies, a material that moved as wind, her bare shoulders battered by light. There was no moon, and the only streetlight in the neighborhood was pecked dead by birds. The light was coming from a cloud of moths, circling her as if she were an open flame.

She stood facing the house for another minute, and then she walked up to the front window, the dark pane like a stilled sea, full of a depth I had never felt. Mariela told me that her mother could divine the future from chicken bones after you'd eaten the meat, that she'd predicted many deaths that way, but that was back when she still spoke. I wondered what she saw in that urn, what she read in the bones. If she'd decided then on silence. If her voice was the easiest thing she could grieve. The moths landed on her shoulders, perching on bone, bright on bright. She took a step back from the window and flew her fist through the glass. It gave like water, her full arm disappearing inside its dark, and the moths veered into the room she'd broken into, soundless as they flew, filling the house to the roof.

Meals for Mourners

Hometown Buffet

On paydays we eat at Hometown Buffet. Mama dresses older to get the senior discount: scab-colored sweater, wool scarf that camouflages the scars on her throat, a broomstick for a cane. She does all this after saying that the white lady at the counter can never tell our age—half of us get the youth discount, and the lady hands us all kids' trays, the ones with walled-off compartments for the entrée and side dish and dessert. My brothers and I strategize beforehand, sketching diagrams of the buffet on our palms and circling our territories with laundry markers: First brother gets entrées, Second and Third and Fourth and Fifth brothers get appetizers, side dishes, salads, and breads, and Sixth brother gets drinks, where he mixes Coke and lemonade into a dark amber mix that Mama calls *a thirsty man's piss*. I man the soft-serve machine. We know the soft serve will make us shit a watery stew, that we'll go home and crowd our only bathroom, bumping asses while all trying to squat over the same toilet bowl. But we eat it anyway, chocolate and vanilla braided together, the two colors slurring to a flesh hue in our bowls. I think it's miraculous, that you can lift a silver lever and make the cream unravel endlessly, an engineered infinity. No one telling me to stop. At home, Mama told me to stop biting my noodles in the middle because it would sever my life short. *I make them long for a reason*, she said. After that, I imagined that the noodles in my mouth were alive, that if I bit one it would burst like a vein, bleed me onto my plate. I started swallowing my noodles whole, tilting my head back to gulp like a fish, until one of my middle brothers told me to stop because it was slutty.

At the buffet, the only table we can fit around is the big one in the center of the crust-carpeted dining room, so everyone watches us eat. My brothers' mouths are heavy machinery, their teeth threshing meat from bone, their tongues endless as conveyor belts.

First brother loves watching the man with an arm-sized knife slice a glazed ham: gloves up to his elbows, the knife a table saw. *I want a knife like that*, he says, and when we ask him what he'd use it for, he says, *I'm going to live in the wild and eat only what I kill.* He is always packing his schoolbag to run away, taking the emergency flashlight from under Mama's bed, Ziploc bags full of raw rice, rope he braided from dental floss, and the Peter Rabbit–printed blanket he shares with Second brother. But he always changes his mind within a few hours, and by that time Mama has already told us to lock all the doors and shut the windows and pin the curtains closed. Sometimes she'll leave him a plate of fish outside the door with no chopsticks and say, *Let him eat like a dog.* I fall asleep waiting by the door and wake to the scrape of his nails against the plate, a pitch higher than prayer. I don't yet know how to name the shame of that sound. I can only wait silently on the other side of his hunger. When Mama finally lets him back in, it's morning and the sky is buttered with clouds. First brother puts everything back in the order he took them, beginning with the flashlight he tucks back under the bed: I see him check the batteries, clicking it on and off as if testing to make sure it'll last till the next time he leaves.

The flashlight is the only thing Baba ever bought for himself. He saw it in a TV ad: a flashlight with a clock embedded in its side that shows military time. Mama asked what the point of the clock was, but Baba could never give a good reason. *Maybe when it's dark,* I said, *you'll need the clock to know how close you are to morning.* First brother laughed and said, *Just look at the sky.* I snuck a box of matches into his backpack—a second source of light—so that he'd never have to see by the light of something stolen.

The flashlight requires twice the batteries and is twice as heavy, the silver barrel so wide around I can't hold it in one hand. Once, Baba found a handprint on the wall. A glowing grease stain that stank of the leftover chicken Mama kept in the fridge. A carcass we all thieved from, kneading the meat between our fingers until it was the temperature of our own flesh. Baba made us all place our hands on the stain, though we already knew whose it matched: First brother was born with hands the size of skillets, too big for his body. Mama always said this meant he'd grow up to be a gambler or a thief. The larger the hands, the greater your gains. The greater your losses. When First brother's hand matched the stain, Baba took the flashlight out from under the bed and beat him till the batteries flew out. The first time he left, First brother flicked on the flashlight and shined it into my face, watching as I winced away. *I just wanted to check if it was broken,* he said.

When the buffet begins to close and we are the last family left, Mama bags our bones. She plucks the gnawed-over drumsticks and harp-shaped wings off our plates, wraps them in napkins, and folds them away in her purse. Later she'll sit in front of the TV and suck the marrow out the way I never learned how, her face white-lit by the soap opera she already knows the end of. Her teeth bungling the bones. When she falls asleep with chicken bones piled like a pyre on her chest, my brothers and I carry her up the stairs. I hold her head. There are seven of us in total, not enough limbs to go around, so two of my brothers walk alongside us as we carry her swinging body.

We love our mother most when she's weightless, divided between our hands. When each of us holds a separate piece of her and thinks we still have time to trade. I know the stories about the miscarriages before us, First brother knows the ones about the zippered scar on her neck, Second brother knows where the gold is kept, Third brother knows why she won't say the word *funeral*, Fourth brother knows exactly whose face is in her newspaper clippings, Fifth brother knows why she keeps the cabinet under the sink locked, and none of us know what exactly Sixth brother knows. To know everything all at once would drown us, so we tread at the level of fact: who, what, when.

Who:

Our mother, forty-nine days after giving birth to me, got a phone call saying that her mother was dead. The last thing Ama had said to her: *Six sons are a winning streak. You can stop now.* I broke the streak and Ama had a stroke.

What:

My mother put me down in the crib and didn't touch me for two days, even when I cried. I was the crime scene. The weapon she didn't know she was carrying. My aunts said I was Ama reincarnated, that her soul had climbed up my spine like a vine, that I lived with two people in my body. They sent phone numbers of shamans to consult over FaceTime, but none of them could confirm who I was.

When:

On the third day, when I was nearly dead, my mother breastfed me. I buttoned my lips to her breast as she wept. Now I eat only salty things, fermented bean sauce and salted duck egg, my mouth acquiring its taste for mourning.

Fig Newtons

The year Second brother lost his memories, Baba gave birth to salt. Baba stayed in the hospital for three days while they cut three salt-stones out of him. The doctor told him to lower his sodium intake, no soy sauce for at least a month. Mama kept the pink-clear stones in a tin can and rattled them once a day, saying it would scare the salt-ghosts away. We asked her what a salt-ghost was and she said it was the spirit of every executed prisoner who was dumped in a river and siphoned back into the sea. My brothers and I took turns cupping the stones in our palms. They were the color of raw salmon and jagged, too sharp for me to hold. I imagined they were still warm from his body, that if I slid one into my mouth it would dissolve and rebuild itself into a diamond inside me.

Mama boiled Coca-Cola with ginger, spooned it hot into Baba's mouth. She said the sugar would cancel out all the salt in his body, and for a whole year she cooked only sweet things, dates stuffed with rice cake, sticky rice with red bean, guava slices rolled in chili-sugar. Second brother bought cans of Coke from the high school vending machine and brought them

home for Mama to boil. At school, his classmates' favorite
game was to ask what he was holding: *Coke,* Second brother
said, pronouncing it like *cock.* His classmates asked again and
again. *Cock-drinker,* they called him. At home, when he asked
me what it meant, I told him that a cock-drinker was someone
who swallowed chickens. In elementary school, there was a
woman who visited every classroom on Easter with a basket of
sun-bleached chicks, letting us cup their throbbing bodies in
our palms. When I told Mama I wanted one of my own, she
ladled chicken-rice stew into my bowl, more marrow than
meat, and said, *That's what a chick grows up to be.* In my mouth,
the rice swelled and thickened into a second tongue. *Eat everything off the bone and maybe you'll birth a chick of your
own.* That night, when I squatted on the toilet, I imagined I
was laying an egg, an animal I could save.

Baba started a fistfight with all the salt in his body. He
punched his belly and crotch to break the salt-boulders inside
him into digestible pebbles. The pain made him miss three
whole days of studying. He was going to be a physicist, he
told us, though he was the oldest person in his class and this
was his third time going back to school. He tried to teach us
all the principles of physics, like *a body in motion stays in motion.* He liked to demonstrate all his lessons: Once, he held
Second brother by his shirt collar and rolled him down our
hardwood staircase. Second brother's body kept going even
after his head bounced off the bottom stair. He slid across our
newly waxed floor and ricocheted off the far wall. Then he
was still, a shadow outlining no body. *A body at rest stays at
rest,* Baba said. Second brother didn't wake up until dinner.
He said he'd dreamed of swimming in a sea made of sugarwater instead of saltwater, that he gave up swimming halfway and started drinking, the sweetness of the water clotting

to sap in his belly. We asked him where he'd been swimming and he said he forgot.

After the car accident on his nineteenth birthday, the first thing Second brother remembered was the time Baba bowled him down the stairs. *A body in motion stays in motion.* When he hit the other car head-on, his body kept moving forward and punched through the windshield. He lolled out like a tongue. The paramedics extracted him from the glass but kept the shard in his belly intact: If they pulled it from him, he'd bleed out in minutes. What was killing him was the same thing keeping him alive.

In the hospital, Second brother ate sweet things: Jell-O cups, instant hot chocolate, over-sugared coffee. Fig Newtons from the vending machine. Baba recognized *Newton* but asked us what *fig* meant. *It's a fruit,* I said, and Baba said, *Did you know an apple discovered gravity?* He told me the story of Newton asleep under an apple tree, how a falling fruit knocked him out of his head and made him famous. At the end of the story, Baba rapped the top of my skull with his closed fist and said, *That's gravity.* For years I thought gravity was when you were knocked in the head. *What happened to your brother?* my classmates would ask, after Second brother went back to school with a bandage swathed around his forehead and jaw. *Gravity,* I said, and they looked at me like I'd been hit too.

Mama slept in a plastic chair by the bed, upright all night. Sometimes we thought Second brother was faking what he forgot, that he really just wanted to stay in the hospital for as long as possible, where the nurses called him handsome and sponged him clean, where the morphine was free. We tried to trick him into remembering: *Cock-drinker,* we said, chanting around his bed. *What's that in your mouth? Cock!* But he always looked at us without recognizing, his pupils dilated to dimes.

The day we left the hospital, we lifted him into the car and his legs felt hollow as bells. On the drive home, I pressed my palms to his eyes so that he wouldn't see the road he'd sped on, the other car coming. I made a night inside his mind. His first day home, he climbed up our stairs with both hands on the railing, wouldn't let go even when he got to the top. *Let go,* I said. Instead, he walked backward, all the way down, still holding on.

Lamb at sea

The story my brothers tell but won't believe: The night Baba left one island for another one, the army patrolled the skin of the shore. No ship could dock safely, so Baba had to swim out to meet it. He had never swum farther than the width of a river, the one that nosed through his city at the speed of concrete. He swam like a dog, paddling his arms, sloshing water into his eyes and mouth until he was salt-sick, gagging.

When he reached the boat, a repurposed British warship, the crew said there was no more room aboard. Baba said he had gold. They threw him a rope, dragged him in. Out of his anus, Baba unraveled a gold-and-pearl necklace. It had been his mother's. The deck was so crowded he walked across bodies to find a spot. Everyone had chosen something different to take: sacks of rare-bred oranges, copies of ancient novels, children. One woman even clung to her favorite goat, its little body bleating with so much grief that another passenger threatened to tear its throat open with her teeth.

Baba claimed that when he got to the island, he only ate three grains of rice at a time to save money. *I didn't shit for a decade,* he said. He even ate the spines of sea urchins boiled translucent, puncturing his belly from the inside. I thought of my father as a balloon with holes. You could blow all you wanted, but it would never become a shape. Baba never cast a shadow. My brothers and I made him stand outside in the sun, posing him in every position like a mannequin, but still he never left behind an outline. *I left my body at sea,* he joked. For a year before he left his hometown, Baba learned how to swim away from soldiers. His mother stood on the riverbank, impersonating a man, her arm aimed like a rifle. *If I can see you, you're dead,* she said, so Baba held his breath and went deep, his mother's voice following him under like a bullet.

The doctor said Baba's body was full of stuck things: salt that wouldn't dissolve into his blood, shit that clogged his gutpipes like leaves in a gutter. When Third brother became a surgeon, Baba became his first patient. In half a lifetime, the salt-stones in Baba's groin expanded into an entire formation, a quarry, a salt-canyon. We all went to the hospital the day of his second surgery, Third brother in his white mask and blue gloves, scrubs, shiny black shoes that made his feet look like dung beetles. Baba was wheeled into the operating room, and Fourth brother was flirting with a nurse in the waiting room. I was the only one who saw:

Third brother, when he was still in medical school, would practice using the scalpel on himself. I once saw him make a diagonal cut on his kneecap and peel the skin back, exposing the bone. It was the whitest thing I'd ever seen, whiter than salt or sugar, so white I didn't know how the body could bear its own purity. His hands shook inside their skin. He stitched his skin back into place and wore long pants for three months.

Bitter melon

Third and Fourth brothers are twins, and even Mama couldn't tell them apart the first few years. Fourth brother dropped out of Mama when she was already back from the hospital, having delivered brother three soundlessly. She walked through the door and he fell out of her like rain. Fourth brother went to medical school too, but then he dropped out and became a waiter after his girlfriend got pregnant.

Mama had been a waitress all her life, even back on the island, where there was no such thing as tipping. The first time she waited in America, at an Applebee's in a neighboring city, another waiter asked her, *How much did he tip you?* And Mama joked, *No, he didn't even touch me.* After Fourth brother became a waiter, Mama refused to speak to him, even over the phone, even after Fourth brother's baby was born so early it crumbled in his fist like paper, its heart too small to carry blood for the whole body. Mama said Fourth brother had soured her heart, that she could have had two doctors for sons but now only had one. Fourth brother sent Mama a whole crate of bitter melons, Mama's favorite, but she wouldn't even look at them.

When the bitter melon didn't un-silence her, Fourth brother sent her a potted orchid made out of plastic. Mama set it on fire in the backyard, the sour smell of singed plastic stalking us into the house.

We heard that after her baby died, Fourth brother's girlfriend stopped eating or drinking, pissing or shitting. Fourth brother kept a collection of syringes to inject fluids into her veins, which turned purple and branched into bruises.

When Second brother said it was better anyway because they couldn't afford to support a family, we all said it was the car accident that turned him cruel. I imagined that his brain was like a bruised apple, a soft black spot breeding itself bigger and bigger until it became the whole fruit.

One night, Fourth brother came to our door after dinner.

He sat with his back to the door until it was nearly morning. Mama finally let him in, and that's when we saw his left hand dangling from his arm like an ornament. When Third brother examined it, he said the bones were broken to breadcrumbs. Mama didn't ask, so we did: Fourth brother said his girlfriend had done it last night with a meat mallet. She was crying while she did it, and he'd been in bed, asleep until the first blow bit into his wrist. The blood was birthed everywhere, soaking through the mattress, and he stayed lying down. He held still while she brought the mallet down harder and harder. Then she put the mallet in the sink and sat down on the ground. Her baby had been smaller than a palm.

Fourth brother went to the ER, but he fled the room as soon as the doctor left to prepare the molding for his cast. *When I'm a doctor,* he used to say to me, *I'll treat everyone for free.* I asked him how he'd pay for his life, and he said, *I'll sell my organs, one by one, until I'm empty.* I imagined him operating on himself, sorting organs into buckets and sewing himself up with nothing but air as his insides. He'd blow away with my breath. I'd be the one who freed him.

Fourth brother passed out when we dragged him through our doorway. Later I'd say he got hit by a car, a story to match Second brother's. It was easier to consolidate injuries that way. Third brother carried him bridal-style to the sofa in our living room, then faked a cast out of cardboard and duct tape. A smell serrated the air, almost bloody, full of garlic: bitter melon soup, a pot of it, my mother stirring and stirring. She broke open the crate and skinned each melon, slitting their pimpled bodies lengthwise. In the pot, the melon-flesh boiled into velvet, the steam erasing her face. My brothers and I ladled gluey melon into bowls, the china pattern faded into bone white, the soup cooling as we sat at the table and waited for Fourth brother to

wake. I was the one who snuck sips of soup until Mama saw
and slapped my wrist. The melons had rotted in the crate, too
syrupy and sweet at the edges, but I swallowed anyway. We ate
through the rot, ate our tongues too, didn't notice until morning when we lisped the same way, none of us able to pray.

Swan meat

Before Mama's throat was slit, she was a singer. Ama sang to
Mama in the womb, curving her head down all the way to her
belly button, cupping her hands around her mouth like a
megaphone. My mother came out of the womb singing: She
didn't cry, just hit a high C until even the doctor applauded.
Fifth brother says this is a lie because Mama wasn't born in a
hospital, because islanders still crawled around like monkeys
back then, because that's what we were before the Dutch and
the Japanese and the general and everyone else: All we did was
eat and grow fur the color of pork floss. But I know the singing
was true. Mama could sing so high only the dogs heard and
came bounding, all of them howling at her door until her father came back with his old pistol and shot each barking bitch
in the throat.

Mama sang on the way to school and back, and all the dogs
that followed her bus into the city got flattened to patties. Her
voice tore silk, watered soil into silt, made the petals weep off
an orchid. It made the sun shy. It made the moon mourn. On
the beach when she sang, the waves lined up at her feet. Boats
sank because the water gave up holding the weight of anything else, too busy listening to my mother, the whole sea on
hiatus.

Fifth brother says this is dogshit and I should stop before
Mama hears: She doesn't like to be reminded of the way the

world once listened to her, all the leaves on the trees blushing into ears. Fifth brother confesses to me that he sings too, that he writes lyrics on the wall with his finger while our brothers sleep, whispering to nothing: *In the city / I was born a night / No one could fall asleep to / In the city / I was born a boy / No one knew was two.*

Two of what? I asked, but he said he hadn't decided yet. I said when he was finished writing, we'd sing a duet together. He held my wrist like a microphone and sang into my fist. In the kitchen, we danced breast-to-breast, so close I thought there were two of myself, his blood chiming in my chest.

Fifth brother says Mama met a lot of famous singers in Taipei, even Teresa Teng. They sang a duet together on TV, and Mama looked at the studio's ceiling the whole time. She imagined her tongue taking flight from her mouth, a recurring nightmare she always had before performing. Her tongue flitted out, thin as a moth's wing, leaving her unable to name its loss.

Fifth brother says there's a photo of our mother and Teresa Teng somewhere, but neither of us asks Mama about it. She wears her scarves even in the shower: checkered wool ones, polka-dotted cotton ones, infinity scarves in colors that scratch at your eyes, yellow and green and pink. Mama always says, *The best way to hide something is to draw attention to it.* One time she hid a bruise by painting her whole face like a skull. It wasn't even Halloween. Baba laughed for two days and said she'd always been a creative woman, able to stage a play out of any pain, make a character out of an injury.

The summer my mother developed vocal nodules, before a doctor slit her throat open to remove the scar tissue, Ama sang at her last funeral. She knew a song for every kind of death. Songs for men who died at war. Songs for women who killed themselves when their men didn't return. Songs for babies who died in the womb. Songs for boys in motorcycle accidents. Songs for girls in basements, buried along abandoned roads, in fields. Songs for triads. Songs for schoolteachers. Songs for exterminators who died from inhaling their own poisons. She was an inventory of grief. She knew every kind of killed, every breed of burial. But people didn't hire professional mourners anymore. Her last funeral was for a man who'd jumped onto a subway track. Ama said she was better at grief than anybody, that she could sing a sadness more real than any widow's. *It's not a real funeral if you don't hire a wailer,* Ama said. Her songs began shallow in the chest, breathy like the beginning of a sob, and then the verses stacked into full shrieks, the lyrics linking into a sky ladder. That's the way Ama would say it. She believed in heaven the way she believed in hands. Years later she found herself sneaking into strangers' funerals, local ones she'd read the announcements for, and when she arrived she was always the oldest person in the room, even older than the body cremated.

In a news report on the death of professional mourning, the majority reported that hiring mourners was redundant. Why burden someone else's body with your own grief? It was invasive, presumptuous for a stranger to stage your sadness. *It's performative,* the interviewees said. Before I was born, Ama watched the report on TV and called Mama about it, her teeth halving peanut shells, producing their own static: *Everything is a performance. Sometimes you need to rehearse your grief so that you come out of it alive. Sometimes you need someone to show you that you can.*

At the end of her last semester in music school, Mama's throat went rigid as bone. Nothing could move through it, out of it. The doctors said she had scars on her vocal cords from using it incorrectly. Mama never thought of her voice as something to use, to wield: She thought of it as a guest, something that was housed in her, a ghost flown into her belly. It was a haunting she welcomed, the way her voice felt both foreign-born and native to her body.

The doctor asked if she'd ever had *invasive surgery* before. Mama said she didn't know what he meant by *invasion*. The same summer she lost her voice, she'd bent over for a boy in the city who told her she sounded like a swan. Mama didn't know what a swan sounded like. She saw them painted on the music boxes they sold in gift shops, but on the island there were only geese that bit your ass. When she went under, Mama's last prayer was that the surgeon slit open her throat but never stitch it back up, leaving her open as a window, the wind scraping through her wick-thin cords. A way she could sing without having to.

Hot Cheetos

Sixth brother was born a fish. Mama says this, but the story lacks proof, the way most do, so we let it stay that way, suspended in the air without ever swallowing it. If Sixth brother had been born a fish, then Mama would have put him in a fish tank instead of the drawer, and he would have outgrown it in a day. He was always growing. There were days when he woke two inches taller, three. One week it was a whole foot. He outgrew Baba by the time he was twelve and I was eleven, but Baba was always hunched anyway, in pain from the salt passing through his bladder. It was also the year Mama stopped being a waitress and started a restaurant with three of my aunts, the Little Shanghai, though none of us had ever been to Shanghai and we were all pretty sure it wasn't little.

My brothers were dishwashers, waiters, cooks, hosts. Even my surgeon brother came at closing time to help stack the chairs on tables and cut new pieces of tablecloth, which was just butcher paper we'd spray-painted gold. Second brother wasn't allowed to count the money. Fourth brother wasn't allowed to flirt with customers. First brother had run away for real this time, though years later some of us swore we'd found his face in the newspaper photo of an investment banker in Macau. We'd argue about the mole on the face in the photo: Had it been over his left eyebrow or the right? None of us had thought to take pictures of him. None of us thought we'd forget his face so thoroughly we'd clip out a picture from the newspaper and pass the thin square back and forth between us so many times that our fingers turned black, a rubbed-off night. Everything we did that day was stained.

Sixth brother's first girlfriend has red fingers. She eats Hot Cheetos for every meal, sometimes dipping them in XO sauce or wrapping them in leftover slices of bread. She leaves red fingerprints everywhere, on the walls of our restaurant and on my brother's skin, his neck, his collar, his fly. The red powder clings to the grooves of her palms, dyes her nails, glitters her lips. My brother, I don't know which one, makes a joke that if we pantsed Sixth brother, there'd be red fingerprints up and down his dick, a red tongue-print. *Worth the burn,* they all say. I pretend to laugh, but I feel like a struck match. I want to set all their spines on fire. Swallow them bottom to top.

Her fingers flit like flames over the customers' plates. We call her Melon because she's round-headed, sweet-bellied. She's only two years older, sixteen when I turn fourteen, but she likes to stroke my cheeks like I'm her child. She comes every day after school to waitress at our restaurant, where Mama pays her below minimum wage and compensates by giving out unsolicited advice about her sons: *Be careful around my second one. Marry the third one. Pray for my first.*

Melon confesses to me that she can never tell my brothers apart, and when I tell them this, they laugh together. After that, the younger ones take turns tricking her: Fifth brother kisses her in the walk-in refrigerator. Fourth brother gives her a bouquet of fake daisies. Fifth brother kisses her again, on the cheek this time, out on the floor where my mother says no touching, no speaking Chinese too loudly to one another, because the customers will think we're bad-mouthing them, no throwing dishes to one another like Frisbees, no running. Every time Melon gets kissed, I look down at the dishes I'm washing and twist the faucet hotter. When my hands emerge from the water quilted with burns, I consider it my punishment. I betrayed her to my brothers, sold them her secret for nothing.

Melon and I take breaks in the parking lot outside the restaurant. She wears a white shirt buttoned up all the way, her collar snug as a bracelet. She has a strong neck, corded and thick, and for a second I wonder if my hands would fit around it. Then I need somewhere new to look, so I look at her mouth, which makes me sweat. I am damp everywhere from wok steam, a heat I mistake for my own. I'm tall enough to wash dishes now, and when my arms ache, Melon massages my wrists until the pulse nearly pounces out of me. In the parking lot, the streetlamp lights only half her face, and I want to drag the sun back out and train it on her like a spotlight. I want to see her wholly in the light or in the dark, unshared by anything. At night when I close my eyes, when the darkness I impose is total, I allow myself to think of her mouth. I circle its shape in my mind, not mine, not mine.

Melon is teaching me to smoke. In the parking lot she lights a cigarette, wincing like it's her own fingertip. She brings it to my lips, but I won't open my mouth. *Trust me,* she says, but I don't know how to say it isn't her I don't trust. I only know how to control my mouth like a cage, opening it to let something out. Never in. When she finally coaxes me into opening by tickling my chin, I won't breathe in. She laughs and says, *Stop holding your breath,* but that only makes me laugh.

What does a boy feel like? I ask her. She turns her face out toward the street. The streetlight shaves away the angles of her face. *Like this,* she says, and presses the lit end of her cigarette into my palm. I don't flinch or cry out. I keep my hands still, the ash hardening to armor. The one time I burned myself in the kitchen, sloshing oil from the wok onto my forearms, Sixth brother strapped a bag of frozen shrimp to each arm. *Keep your arms above your head,* he said. *The hurt will flow down to your feet and exit your body.* When I locked myself in the bathroom to cry, Sixth brother knocked on the door with his elbow, his hands carrying a still-hot pot. *Do you need me to amputate you?* he asked, trying to make me laugh. I said it wouldn't matter anyway: Pain outlives the body. I told him about phantom limbs, how a feeling can be attached to nothing, how memory is meat. He didn't believe me.

When she can't get me to smoke, Melon and I play our embarrassing-story game. The rules are one: Tell an embarrassing story. Melon always reuses the same stories, but I never mind. They're a little different every time, and my own private game is to trace what's changed and guess why. Today she tells me yesterday's: *One time I used a stick of imitation crab as a tampon. Then I put it back in the bag. When we had hotpot that night, my brother asked why he tasted blood in the broth. I said something must have died in it.* The difference is that there's a brother in the story when I know she doesn't have one. I think she knows my brothers have been tricking her. I think she's sampling them, testing the temperature of their mouths, the weight of their hands on her waist, their eyes always watching her, even when she isn't there. She takes their eyes with her, carries them home and into our parking lot. Flips them like coins. Juggles them invisibly. I feel them even now, eyes like pebbles in my pockets.

When Sixth brother and I were too young to know our bodies, Mama bathed us together in the sink. She stirred up bubbles with dish soap, whisking the water frothy with her hands, folding boats made of newspaper. Sixth brother played the wind, blowing into the black-and-white sail, and I was the sea, churning my hands below the surface to make the water wave. We hadn't seen the ocean yet, but it was instinct: the air and water both moving, above and below, sometimes in tandem and sometimes opposite, the waves pulling back like reins. When the boat was too soaked to remember its shape, it sank, and my brother cried. I watched the paper dissolve, black ink spooling into the water and across it, spanning the sink like a new skin. I didn't cry. I knew it wasn't a real boat, a real sea. I knew not to mourn what had never been born.

Back then, Mama was worried that I never cried: She nearly starved me because I didn't cry for milk. She slept with me balanced on her belly, until Baba complained and she put me back in the drawer buffered with blankets, the same one my brothers were raised from, the same one I used to dream was a boat full of holes, though my brothers say there's no way, I would've been too young to remember my dreams. I asked them if they remembered when I was born and they said, *Of course.* I wanted to say I remembered their births too, but that was impossible. They had happened behind me, beyond me. And still I felt like I'd been witness to their beginning, that I'd birthed them myself or been born into each of them. Sometimes I saw my own mouth grinning around Second brother's teeth or grew a nose parallel with Third brother's, and each time I forgot it was because we all shared a common denominator, and not because I had sprung from them alone, my father-mothers, my brothers.

The embarrassing story I tell Melon is this: When I was born, I became my grandmother, but without the voice, the ability to make a history out of hurt. When I turned ten, Mama said it was time to expel Ama from my body. But I didn't get why Ama had to leave me. *There are certain things you can't grow up to be,* Mama said. *You can't grow up to be someone else.* I said, *What about myself?* and Mama said, *You can't be that either.* I wanted to ask, *Then what?*

What:

I tell Melon I once believed a life could be written like a lyric, beginning to end.

Who:

Melon shakes her head and says I think too much about music when I should be thinking about meat. We spend the evening snipping the skin off raw chickens, parsing tendon from fat from talon. She says the hens are impossibly ripe in this country, bigger than our heads, and I say it's because they've mutated, bred to outweigh what their bones can support.

When:

The first time Melon kisses me, she tugs me behind someone's parked car, a minivan with a dog in it. I watch the dog pawing the window, its tongue pulsing against the glass like the overcrowded fish at the grocery store, their scaled bodies thudding against the tank as they try to swim away from their kin. Afterward, when we return to the restaurant, Melon hums the rest of the day, a blank sound no one can name. I begin to suspect that Melon has stolen my breath and is singing with it.

Where: in the parking lot, again. Again

again.

Mama says every song begins as breath, every hole knows how to sing. The mouth, the anus. All of it is wind in the body. After Ama had her stroke and died, after her ashes were sent to California in a cardboard box and Mama ordered an urn and lid online, after I was born with Ama lodged in the shaft of my throat, a canary warning me of myself, Mama sang to us.

It was an old mourning song, the kind with lyrics that could not be written, only steeped in the body and poured out through the mouth. After her surgery, Mama's voice was metallic, flint striking stone. It entered the kitchen like a light source. It burned us fleshless, listening like that. We were bone to bone.

The song ended and we were all smoke. Because Mama didn't want to pay the cemetery to swallow Ama's ashes, she kept the urn in her closet for years. We told her it was bad luck, but she said we could never delineate ourselves from the dead. Then she moved Ama's urn to the drawer under the sink. In the kitchen, we stood in a row and bowed three times to it. I asked Sixth brother if he remembered when we were both small enough to fit in that sink, to get clean in it. He said nothing, but the silence was its own body. It fit between us. It was our secret sibling. Mama shut the cabinet door under the sink and we went back to breathing. In the throat-dark of her urn, Ama's ashes sang back. The cabinet began to leak song, a frantic beat like wings flapping, but when Mama opened the door there was nothing. At night we listened to the song for hours, counting the notes until we fell asleep, the night noised by wings, a heartbeat under the sink. But eventually we gave up trying to measure the lifespan of that sound. We let it outlive us. We let it tell us our names.

Acknowledgments

The following stories have appeared in different forms: "Auntland" (*Sine Theta Magazine*), "The Chorus of Dead Cousins" (*McSweeney's Quarterly Concern*), "Mandarin Speakers" (*DREGINALD*), "Eating Pussy" and "Homophone" (*New Delta Review*), "Nine-Headed Birds" (*VIDA Review*), "Dykes" (*Sinister Wisdom*), "Meals for Mourners" (*Nashville Review*).

Endless gratitude to my agent Julia Kardon for her guidance and her humor. To Hannah Popal and everyone on the HG Literary team for their support. To my wonderful editor Nicole Counts for her empathy, insight, generosity, and understanding, and for seeing the core of these stories and guiding me toward the wild and curious. To Oma Beharry, Chris Jackson, and the entire One World team for all their hard work and for making this book possible. To Kathy Lord and Dennis Ambrose for their copyediting expertise and guidance. To Grace Han for designing a transformative, world-rearranging, gasp-inducing cover, and to Michael Morris for his art direction. To Jo Anne Metsch for making the inside of this book look so beautiful and alive. To Mikaela Pedlow and everyone at Harvill Secker for giving these stories a home in the UK. To everyone at Hanser Berlin for allowing my stories to travel and take flight. To my writing group: Amy Haejung, Pik-Shuen Fung, Kyle Lucia Wu, and Annina Zheng-Hardy, for their brilliance and kindness, and for tolerating my disclaimers. To Maya, for her humor and friendship, for tolerating my extremely panicky messages about commas, and for eating Hot Cheetos on benches with me. To Rattawut Lapcharoensap, whose class provided the inspiration, motivation, and sense of wonder that allowed me to write these stories. To all the literary magazine editors who ushered these stories into the world, and to everyone who read them. To all my friends. To my family, who showed me how to tell stories and how to laugh.

PHOTO: TRINA QUACH

K-MING CHANG is a Kundiman fellow, a Lambda Literary Award finalist, and a National Book Foundation 5 Under 35 honoree. She is the author of *Gods of Want* and *Bestiary*, which was longlisted for the Center for Fiction First Novel Prize, the PEN/Faulkner Award, and the VCU Cabell First Novelist Award.

kmingchang.com

To inquire about booking K-Ming Chang for a speaking engagement, please contact the Penguin Random House Speakers Bureau at speakers@penguinrandomhouse.com.